THE DA
VINI R
& OTHER STORIES

WILL KEMP
JANE McLAUGHLIN
KATE MITCHELL
with
JANE AUSTIN
JENNIFER BAILEY
ROSA CAMPBELL
AOIFE FITZPATRICK
MANDY HUGGINS
KATHRYN LUND
L F ROTH

selected by JEREMY WORMAN

JAN FORTUNE (editor)

INDEPENDENT INNOVATIVE INTERNATIONAL

Published by Cinnamon Press,
Meirion House,
Tanygrisiau,
Blaenau Ffestiniog,
Gwynedd
LL41 3SU
www.cinnamonpress.com

ISBN 978-1-910836-19-4
British Library Cataloguing in Publication Data. A CIP record for
this book can be obtained from the British Library.

Designed and typeset in Garamond by Cinnamon Press. Cover
design by Adam Craig.

Cinnamon Press is represented by Inpress
and by the Welsh Books Council in Wales.

Printed in Poland

Introduction

The most recent Cinnamon Press short story prize saw our largest number of entries and a huge range of themes and styles, giving Jeremy Worman a considerable task in selecting the final winners and runners up. *The Day I Met Vini Reilly* represents the best entries, with fine examples of work from a group of emerging writers to look out for.

Jeremy Worman writes:

A striking feature of the shortlisted stories was their range and ambition, for example: a fictionalized piece about the Piltdown Man hoax; the impact on a child of her prostitute mother; the suicide of a father, and much more.

Francine Prose makes the point that 'Great writers painstakingly construct their fictions with small but significant details that, brushstroke by brushstroke, paint the picture the artist hopes to portray [...] of which they hope to convince us.' The best stories here knew when to pause the action, to emotionally and visually intensify through detail, but also when to move on, so as not to dilute, or divert, the central focus of the text. 'Face Values', for instance, is a touching story in which a girl moves from resentment to respect for her father, but it is diminished by an opening paragraph that tells too many details, without leaving emotional space for the reader to imagine the scene, and the paragraph tips into melodrama. Such small technical oversights often made the difference between those stories selected for the anthology and those not.

Endings are the key structural feature of a short story, the point to which writer and reader are urged, and the promontory from which the reader looks back to test if the shock, or surprise, of the ending has been justified, but also gazes forward into the unknown future. Many very good stories, 'Fair Game' for example, just missed out on an anthology place because the ending did not quite manage to raise the level of drama necessary to a really convincing conclusion.

I want to make another tentative distinction between those excellent stories in the anthology and the very good ones on the shortlist: those in the anthology exhibited more confidence in the narrative voice of the story. I trusted the writer because I was won over not only by the plot but by the authority of the writing. This was their story and they knew just how to tell it. I often gained this first crucial impression by the end of the first paragraph.

Joyce Carol Oates makes a shrewd point about the short story: 'My personal definition of the form is that it represents a concentration of imagination, and not an expansion.' Each of the stories in the anthology fulfilled this condition and the three winners did it with particular flair.

'The Day I Met Vini Reilly' by Will Kemp has a pop buzz feel from the outset as the male narrator, an infatuated fan, sets off to see a gig by his hero Vini Reilly, guitarist and leader of the Manchester band The Durutti Column, formed in 1978. The reader is absorbed into the enthusiasm of the author. Light-touch social commentary, ironic personal reflections, sharp dialogue and insights about the author and his hero, fuse history and autobiography to create a bravura narrative that rescues from obscurity a cultural and personal moment.

In 'Common Ground' by Jane McLaughlin the solitude of the narrator, living in a country cottage after the breakup of a relationship, is striking for its ironic lack of self pity. The originality comes not from further self analysis but through meeting a travellers' family who have made an encampment at the edge of her land. She is drawn further into their life and through helping them, in a highly charged conclusion, finds a kind of emotional release for herself.

The dramatic first paragraph of 'Eclipsed' by Kate Mitchell really grabbed my attention: a successful middle-aged couple, barristers, are on a cruise ship when a young man comes to their dinner table and says hello to the woman, with whom he has had an affair. The social and psychological entanglement is well drawn out, the dialogue and details crisp and controlled, as the story skilfully constructs the various elements to bring the narrative to a chilling conclusion.

'Driving Blind' by Jennifer Bailey is set in a tense urban environment and this well controlled story tells of the emotional drama between a father, his grown-up daughter and their strange neighbour Michael, which twists to a satisfying ending.

'Restoration' by Aoife Fitzpatrick has a tone reminiscent of William Trevor and the first-person voice of an elderly uncle reveals, through strongly felt imagery, unresolved family feelings after the death of his sister.

'This Is For You' by L.F. Roth is a psychological story of a woman who reflects on the trauma caused by her piano lessons as a girl and reaches a taut yet subtle climax.

'Pink Knickers' by Mandy Huggins is a cheeky, touching narrative about a moment of teenage romance that has unforeseen consequences and delivers in the ending what is promised at the start.

'Les Petites Curies' by Jane Austin is written in the first-person voice of Madame Curie's daughter; set in 1914 France, it combines historical and personal drama to great effect.

'Whatever Happened To Sarah-Jayne?' by Kathryn Lund is a daring, experimental, funny, Kafkaesque story that traces and undermines the identity, or non identity, of Orson as he disappears.

The international feel of 'From Where You Are In The Machine' by Rosa Campbell, set in contemporary hi-tech Saigon, about a couple's complex relationship, intriguingly weaves together social, personal and historical narratives.

Contents

Common Ground
Jane McLaughlin

No one comes here, except the delivery vans, an occasional builder trying to drum up business, and the post. Not that there is much of that. There's a good connection and everything online.

It still surprises me how easy it is for me to live like this.

It was only meant to be for a few weeks. Just to have a space, to put some time and distance between my old life and whatever was going to happen next.

A common enough story. Betrayal, discovery, destruction. People go through it every day. But it demolished me in a way I could never have predicted. Me, the successful professional woman, always up for a challenge or new venture. A supportive, creative partner, helping me to do whatever I wanted. And lying every inch of the way.

I found this place. A haven complete with wagtails and thrushes. A cottage, sweet as gingerbread, the curve of the slates on the roof lapping over each other in a little wave pattern, a shiny blue door, the squares of the window panes polished like crystal. As in a romantic English watercolour, it stands at the confluence of two pretty streams, flanked by watermeadows where sheep graze, and beyond that, low wooded hills. I sank into it like a deep pool, a place where the life before had no meaning.

When I first came I had no time, I did not count days or even know which day of the week it was. I would wake in the night and stay up till dawn, then sleep in the garden half the day.

As the days unfolded I began to do the things that the place asked me to do—small tasks of gardening, cleaning, repairing. These gave me little patterns to follow, when the big one made no sense.

People would ask ring me, ask when was coming back, and I would say 'Soon' but never put a date on it. And the date never came. I had everything I needed. I could work online. I could go out in the morning and sit by the stream and listen to the birds and the sound of water. Sometimes the sound of a tractor in the distance or the crack of a bird scarer, but nothing to threaten or disturb my mind. Because there were still deep bruises that had not surfaced, feelings that I could not bear to visit.

So I found no reason to leave. 'In a good place', people say. I could only think of places that would be worse.

I was grateful for peace, if happiness was not possible.

Until one sunny June afternoon.

I was trimming straggling branches out of the beech hedge when I heard the sound of a vehicle approaching. By this time I knew well the sound of the few delivery vans that came down the track and it was a hoarse rattly note that definitely wasn't one of them.

I looked up and saw that it was something of a convoy. Two rather old and battered cars, one of them pulling a trailer caravan, and a white transit van. They bumped off the track and over the unshorn grass to a small promontory of land that was looped round by one of the streams. They drew up in a line and turned off the engines.

There was a pause. Then a man and a woman and two children got out of one of the cars. The woman had blonde hair and was very pregnant. The men were both dark—one tall, one shorter. They opened up the door of the trailer, propped it open and let down the stairs so that they rested on the grass. They began to unload some kitchen items and some children's toys.

Gypsies. Tinkers. Travellers. Pikeys. Or whatever the politically correct or incorrect description is these days.

I felt afraid. I feared the destruction of the calm I treasured so much. I was afraid of how I might have to be. Would I have to be Angry Resident, complaining vociferously about rubbish dumped in my garden and non-biodegradables being thrown into the stream? This was more than I could do.

And I thought: these people may be escaping too. Life on the road could not be easy. If they wanted peace and calm they had as much right to it as I. But my head filled with the newspaper stories of chaos and noise.

The bank where they had pulled up was common land, the farmer's fence was fifty yards away. For the moment they were out of the sightline from most of my windows and until I went out of my garden I could probably pretend that they were not there.

For the next few days I tried to do just that. But I took surreptitious glances over the hedge, or wandered down to the bank of the stream, keeping an eye on them as I went. One of the cars and the two men seemed to be absent most of the time. When they were there, they seemed to spend most of their time with their heads under one of the cars, feet stuck out on the grass. When they did that, they kept the car radio on loud, blasting music across the fields.

Apart from that they didn't seem to be making much noise or rubbish. Then the men seemed to disappear completely. I saw the blonde woman from time to time, hanging out the washing or moving with her flat-footed pregnant gait between the van and the trailer. Once I heard her singing.

Then one day I was pruning the roses and turned round to see that someone was watching me.

A small girl with blonde hair was standing on the crosspiece of my wicket gate, holding on to two of the uprights, her feet in pink trainers stuck between them at the bottom. She was wearing a pink T shirt with 'Babe' inscribed on it in diamanté letters. Her blonde hair was pulled up into a little fountain on top of her head with a mauve artificial flower attached to the elastic holding it together. She was staring at me with little expression in her eyes. Behind her was a smaller boy, also watching me, hands stuck into the pockets of his baggy jeans.

I tried to carry on pruning as if she was not there, but it was hard to ignore the stare. After a few minutes I then turned to her.

'Hello. What's your name?'

She did not answer, but continued to stare, apparently at the distance behind me.

I waited for a reply. As none came, I turned back to my pruning.

After a few minutes I heard a voice behind me.

'Tara.'

'What did you say?'

'Tara'

'Is that your name?'

She stuck her thumb in her mouth and nodded. The child behind her continued to stare unblinkingly, hands still in his pockets.

'Hello Tara. Do you live over there?'

She nodded.

'Is your mum going to have a baby?'

'Goss. He's gone up Faversham for the cars. With Barry.'

'Is Barry your Dad?'

There was a silence.

'Goss. If the baby comes, she has to phone Goss.'

'Where will she go when the baby comes? To hospital?'

She shook her head.

'To the shop. The shop where they get babies. Goss will take her to get it.'

'What's your mum's name?'

'Goss.'

'The same as your Dad?'

'Terry Goss. Her name Terry Goss.'

'And is that your brother?'

'That's Tyrone. He's got to learn to behave.'

With that she took a backward leap from the gate, clasped the hand of the boy behind her and ran off towards the trailer.

I watched them go, a little envious of the way their little limbs covered the ground, flying over the tussocky grass until they tumbled up the stairs of the trailer.

The next day the men were back, doing more work on the car. I was trying to work. The noise was very loud. After an hour of it, the noise of the shrill music drilling into my head, I steeled myself to walk over. Don't be angry, I said to myself, don't be self-righteous, it won't help. Don't be Angry Resident, they have seen too much of that. But they have to understand that other people live here too.

I crossed the grassy field between my cottage and their encampment. As I drew near I noticed some odd bits of machinery lying about haphazardly but nothing too unpleasant. What I could see of the trailer through the open door looked clean and there was bright washing strung from it on a line run to a stake in the ground.

I approached the car, but the noise of the radio blasting out masked any sound of my approach. There was one pair of feet sticking out from under the car. I did not feel like jogging a foot to attract attention. So I just bent down and tried to look under the car. He must have noticed the change in the light this caused, and slid out from underneath. He lay there, suddenly at a loss, as he clearly had not expected to see a strange woman standing over him. He was the smaller of the two dark-haired men. He looked at me with dark uncomprehending eyes, more surprised than angry. Realising that he might feel his position put him at a disadvantage, I backed off a few feet while he got up. Standing up, he was slightly taller than myself, wearing old jeans and an oily sweatshirt.

'Mr Goss?'

He made a sideways movement with his head, as if to say, he might be.

'I'm glad to meet you Mr. Goss.'

I was not going to be branded a gypsy-hater. I held out my hand.

He wiped the oily hand on the side of his jeans and touched mine, lightly, his expression something like mockery.

He had a tanned, slightly crooked face.

'Well, princess, what can I do for you?'

Princess! The cheek of it. No one had ever called me that before. I'm a professional woman. When I worked for the company, anyone who'd done that would have been out on their ear.

The radio was still blaring out.

'Mr Goss, I really don't want to be difficult but I'm trying to work over there.'

'Oh yes?'

'The noise, I mean. I work in my house. I was wondering if you could keep the noise down a bit.'

'The noise. See, we're working on the car. Makes a bit of noise, can't help you there.'

'I mean the radio.'

14

'My radio only does loud. Can't turn it off at the moment. I'm trying to fix it.'

I gave him what I hoped was an authoritative look.

'I'd be really grateful if you could do that. There are laws about noise now.'

Something in the air seemed to attract his attention and he looked upwards. Then gave me a sidelong look and dived under the car again.

I realised that the woman had come to the door of the caravan. She was standing on the top stair, looking at me. She was dressed in trousers and a green T shirt pulled over her large bump, now looking even more imminent. She had a face that seemed to combine a kind of prettiness with rough cut features. She too had blonde hair pulled up in a topknot like Tara's. I waved at her but she did not respond and I turned to go back to my cottage.

To be fair, the noise did seem to moderate a little. In the evening everything was quiet. I got up early the next morning, a perfect midsummer dawn with dew sparkling across the gossamer on the grass, and Goss's car was gone.

Neither he nor the other man returned for several days. And all was quiet. From time to time I caught sight of Mrs Goss hanging out washing or sometimes just standing on the bank of the stream while the children played on the bank. Yes, the caravan and the other vehicles were a bit of an eyesore, but sometimes the figures on the bank of the stream looked like an idyllic eighteenth-century genre painting. Sometimes Tara would come back to stand on my gate, and pass the time of day with me. She did not seem to have much knowledge of a child's world, but she knew how adults live and how to talk to them. She knew a lot of place-names in Kent and Essex. She liked places with rivers best.

So it was quiet, until the Wednesday afternoon, that is.

For the first time, Tara opened my gate and ran into my house through the door standing open. She looked distressed.

She gripped my arm and fixed her dark-blue eyes on me. For a while she didn't seem able to say anything. She wasn't crying, but she looked as if she might. She hung on to me even tighter. I wanted to push her off. I liked Tara when she was chirpy and chatty. I didn't like this clinging creature. I've never pretended to have much in the way of maternal instinct. At last she said:

'Terry's crying because of the baby.'

'Has the baby come?'

'No, but she's crying. She says it's coming out.'

'Where's your dad then? Hasn't she phoned him?'

Her face tightened into anxiety and her grip on my arm felt like panic.

'Her phone isn't working.'

I stared at her. Obviously, I would have to go over there with my own mobile and get her husband to come back. Much as I would have liked to, I couldn't let these people sort out their own problem. If they didn't have a working phone at a time like this...but I'm not inhuman and could not leave them to get on with it.

In the caravan I could see Terry lying on the sofa built along the wall. There seemed to be lace curtains everywhere. Her face was red and she was indeed crying uncontrollably. As a contraction came her sobs turned to a kind of throaty roar. She twisted and turned on the sofa. The dead phone was lying on the floor at her side.

'I'll get your husband to come—what's his number?'

She pointed tearfully at the phone lying on the floor.

'Can't you remember it?'

She shook her head and launched into another intense contraction.

Obviously the labour was far advanced. There was a woman in here about to give birth, and I was the only person who could do anything about it.

But I knew I couldn't. I used to battle six crises a day and then go down the gym and a late film. I had nothing left now. I needed to put myself back together before I had to cope with other people.

I stood immobile on the caravan floor. I could not move. Then Terry reached out and grabbed my hand.

She said 'Now! You must take me now!'

An autopilot went on.

I ran back across the grass and started my car, and drove back across the bumpy ground. I shoved the children into the back and somehow heaved Terry down the steps and into the front seat. As we bumped back across the grass she screamed in pain. The children crouched on the back seat, terrified. I should have got them into seatbelts, but for the moment I could only concentrate on one thing. Getting Terry to the hospital.

I was angry. I was angry with the men who had gone off and left her. I was angry that these people had intruded onto my territory and then made me take part in their miserable drama. I was angry with Terry for being incompetent and difficult and now for being noisy and uncontrollable. It seemed dangerous even to try driving with her thrashing about in the front of the car. Something terrible was going to happen to some if not all of us.

I found it hard to control my hands, but turned on the satnav and pushed the 'nearest hospital' button. Metherden General Hospital, six miles away.

The mechanical voice sent me westwards, along the lane to the main road.

As I stopped at the turning I looked at Terry, her small twisted face, her topknot of blonde hair and I did not feel angry any more. I suddenly felt something like love for this tormented woman. As if her raging emotions had charged my own empty battery. The only important thing in the world now was to make sure that her baby came into the world alive and intact.

The roads to Metherden were small and quiet. For once there was no hay lorry or tractor to hold us up.

Then suddenly she gave a scream and blood spurted into the car. What looked like fountains, streams of it pouring on to the floor. I had no idea blood could come out like that, in such quantities.

I stopped, pulled as far as I could on to the verge. There were open fields on either side.

'I'm dying, I'm dying' she screamed and I was afraid she was right. She began to scream curses about Goss, wishing him more terrible things than I could imagine.

In these moments they say you lose all sense of time. I can remember dialling 999 and trying to tell the person on the phone how far I was from the last village and trying to staunch the blood with the rug from the back of the car. I can't say how many minutes it was before the blue lights appeared, the siren sounding, and suddenly man and women in yellow tabards were pulling out stretchers, and all kinds of machinery and drips. By that time Terry was losing consciousness. They shot her into the ambulance as if, as it truly was, a matter of life and death. A police car arrived and a policewoman picked up the children and carried them tenderly, rigid with fear, into the car and drove away.

I was left at the roadside with my blood-soaked car. I sat in it and cried for half an hour. Fuck them I thought, how dare they. How dare they invade my beautiful space, dump their problems on me and ruin my smart car. How dare they. How dare *he* leave his wife in that state. As I sat and sobbed in my car a few drivers in tractors and cars looked at me enquiringly but none of them stopped. I drove to the nearest pub, had three large brandies and got a taxi home.

When I woke up, it was late at night. There was bright moonlight shining on the water and owls calling from the woods. One of them, white and ghostly, flew straight over the house. A bad omen, I wondered? I telephoned the hospital. They would tell me nothing.

I cried among the roses in my moonlit garden. Round the side of the house I caught site of the little parked colony, lightless, silent. I cried again, it looked so sad.

I woke again in the late morning and they had gone. My view across the stream and the fields was as uncluttered as ever. I knew I would never see them again. If I really wanted to, I might be able to contact them through the police, but I knew I would not do that. They had gone, not wanting to see me or thank me, and I would never know if the mother and the baby survived to travel on elsewhere, with the two blonde children who would never hang on my gate again.

When I went to pick up the post, there was a used brown envelope taped up with sellotape on it lying on the mat.

There was a name written on it: Kiera Goss.

Kiera. A girl.

There was something heavy inside it. When I opened it, a heavy gold neck-chain fell out, with a large gold coin hanging from it. The inscription on the coin was in some kind of Cyrillic alphabet. The gold looked old and worn, as if it was somebody's heirloom.

From where you are in the machine
Rosa Campbell

The sleeping and the sleepless have nothing in common, thinks Jiang, watching Tranh sleep, fitful in her glittering tower. Thinks Tet, standing on the veranda, the gum trees rustling their silver leaves around her. Both wait for the breaking day.

Jiang lies tiny in the huge white bed she shares with her new husband. Her bedroom is one of the one hundred and fifty identical gleaming bedrooms of the Saigon Pearl, where she is kept well by Tranh, the air conditioner he just bought for her keeps her company after he leaves for work. She pads silently to the living room.

Tranh calls her Little Cat because of that slinky way she walks. The first time he called her that was when they met for cocktails at Sky bar, that western-style place he likes. They stood at the floor to ceiling window and he put his hand on her back, finding her damp skin through the folds of her green dress. He pointed out the apartment block she now stands in.

'See that? Count four across, twenty up, that's where I live.' She found the forth flat on the twentieth story. The light was on and she wondered if he'd left it glowing for her. He seemed impulsive—he'd got there slightly late with the top button of his shirt undone. She liked that, liked the way he threw his shiny keys to his motorbike down onto the table. But maybe he had mapped it all out. Had he planned to guide her through the view?

He read her mind, 'My maid is there now, cleaning.'

He pointed out the four factories around the apartment. 'They're mine, too.' The windows of the factories burned fluorescent, lit up against the pollution from the ring road.

'Why are the lights still on?' she asked.

Tranh laughed, 'Welcome to the new Saigon.'

'Plastics?'

'Not a pretty face, eh,' he said in English, impressed.

'Do you mean me?' She asked in Vietnamese, 'Because if you do, you mean,' and here she switched to English not waiting for him to answer, 'not *just* a pretty face.'

He hadn't expected this and she liked that more than anything else so far. She wanted to comfort him and laugh at him at the same time with his new Saigon swagger.

She switched back to Vietnamese, 'Or do you mean, your factories, in which case you would say, 'Not a pretty *sight*.'

Then Jiang the cat walked slinkily to the bar and Tranh was left to scrape his jaw off the floor.

Later, after more dates and many more drinks, he would get his own animal nickname; rabbit. Because of the small tuft of hair on his lower back, like a fluffy bunny tail she said. Really though it was because he'd been so shocked on the first date, like that other English expression, rabbit in headlights.

She envies her rabbit this morning though sleeping soundly. She stands at the door and looks at him, stretched out on the enormous bed. When he's awake he's so worried that she can't sleep, but his sleeping self betrays him. He likes that she can't do it. He likes the big bed all to himself. Fucking show off, she thinks, turning away.

She says hello to the Grandparents on the altar. Her Grandmother says 'oh, still not sleeping, hey?' Her

Grandfather smiles and chews his betel. She lights two sticks of incense, as a gift, to shut them up. Her grandfather smiles wider.

She nuzzles into the enormous L-shaped couch and flicks on MTV Asia, choice of this or the Communist Party so early. She turns the sound off. K-pop style Vietnamese bands dance silently. The sun starts to touch the windows of the factories, where the lights are always on, always working, always sleeping, never stopping. The factories her husband owns where it is always relentless day.

Tet stands on her veranda. People make a big deal of sunrise, she thinks. They go on package holidays to see it, request wake-up calls, set alarms on extra loud and still some of them sleep through. Awake and alone she has seen the sky go from fairy floss pink, to orange, dip-died through to blue rising up over Melbourne hundreds of times.

Unlike Jiang, it's been like this for Tet since that day in February when she squirmed out of Barry's cuddle and ran with a fat legged pitter-patter in nothing but a purple cloth nappy. She ran out to the back yard and spun round and round until she fell down on the lawn. The summer air was fragrant with peppercorn tree. The buffalo grass tickled her tiny baby version of Julie's nose. She heard her mother and father inside laughing, heard Barry cracking an after work beer and Julie having a sip. Through the window they kissed each other, admired their glorious child entertaining herself on the lawn. As the sky stilled itself above Tet she thought, there can be no better game than this. Nothing is better than making the sky go round and round and then falling down dizzy with the whirling blue inside you.

Inside, Jules pulled the leaves off basil for pesto and Barry washed the grease off his hands with soap made from tar. The water gurgled sudsy black down the sink on this day like any other in the mid–1980s, until Tet screamed from the backyard. The grownups ran, carrying a look of shock to Tet. Blood streamed down her chin, down her little chest and baby belly. Julie pinched Tet's wound shut with her two fingers.

At the hospital, Barry nicked out for a smoke and Julie paced the lino in her sandals, held her baby girl against her sweaty body. They sewed up Tet's chin with six neat black stitches and her mother thought, my baby was perfect and now she's not. The world has begun to grasp my Tet with its sharp claws.

Julie used to put her down by giving her a feed and reading Tet's favourite book, *Digging for Honey Ants*. But after the accident Tet started pointing to the stitches on her face and then pointing to the ants, panicked, unable to nap.

'I think that book's maybe making it hard for her to have a kip, Jules,' said Barry when he got home from work. 'I reckon she thinks she's got ants on her face.'

'I guess you're right mate. It would make it pretty hard to nod off.'

He sucked the metal mouth of his beer, 'Too bloody PC anyway that book, maybe you should read her something different.'

Jules scowled at him, 'Maybe you should quit your job and learn to breast feed then you can read her Cinderella till the cows come home.'

Tranh rummages for coffee, startling Jiang out of the place between awake and asleep that she is drifting in, drifting on the bright colours of MTV and the sun waking Saigon. Jiang logs that. Another example of him

23

not caring that she can't sleep. She sits up drowsily, watches the neighbours on the tower block across bring in their washing. This is what normal people who sleep do isn't it, these kind of everyday things? Put out the washing, take it in. But Tranh doesn't want to hang their washing outside, says it's too polluted. 'The air looks the same but it's not,' he said when she tried. He bought her a dryer.

'Can you make me a coffee too please?'

'Sure! Do you want extra milk, baby?' The question is code for are you still not sleeping?

She nods. OK, so maybe he does care a little.

Since this wave of insomnia crashed over Jiang and Tranh and their new fledgling marriage, she's been taking her coffee with extra condensed milk, the more the better, to keep her going for what will probably be the next twenty four hours and the next twenty four hours after that, and on and on till who knows when.

While the coffee brews, he sits down and puts an arm around her, 'Sorry, little cat that you're not sleeping. Is there anything I can do? Maybe ginseng? Something from the market? New pillows, I can order them online if there's something you want that we can't get here?'

Jiang's eyes well up. Her Grandmother shoots her a disapproving look from the altar;

'You're so soft hearted! You need to toughen up! You're just like your grandfather.' Her Grandfather is silent, just as he used to be when she'd admonish him when they were alive.

He'd get up from the table in the small flat where they lived and shuffle onto the street or leave the market stall where they worked, away from her insults. He would come back a couple of hours later with a small gift for her Grandmother, wrapped sweets, oranges, some cherry blossom flowers tied with a red bow and all would be forgotten.

They suck their coffees down greedily. She enjoys this ritual they keep up, coffee before work is normal. Jiang likes normal.

'Busy day ahead?' she asks.

'Yeah, new contracts with the US and Australia have come through. Changed from China to us, we're cheaper, better.'

'Well done.'

Tranh grins, pleased at her praise, 'Try to sleep little cat.'

'I'm sure I will.'

Maybe this will be the day that the miracle of sleep will wash over her.

Tet sucks up a mug of coffee too, gets as much in as she can before she begins her day at Smart Chef, though there is no clear beginning, no clear end. She spent last night as she does most nights, sourcing the cheapest furniture and containers online. Instead of sleeping, she gets in touch with suppliers. This gives her an edge on the competition.

Tet started Smart Chef in 2009, widely acknowledged as the worst time to start a business in seventy years. But Tet turned the crisis into an opportunity. She noticed the restaurants in her neighbourhood were drawing their awnings with a sigh. New restaurants couldn't open, couldn't risk the start up costs. So, Tet thought, I'll rent restaurants, everything they need, if they go broke, which many of them will, I'll charge them a fee and rent the stuff to someone else.

Barry hit the roof; he practically lurched for the Marx on the bookshelf. 'You'll get rich on others failures.'

Julie interrupted him, 'You're doing yourself no favours my love.' She turned to Tet, 'It's your life,' she said, meaning, this is not the way we raised you. This is not what we wanted you to want; this is not the future we dreamed up for you. Meaning, between us reading you dreamtime stories and singing Bread and Roses over your cot, between the Steiner pre-school and the good public high school we fought to get you into so you wouldn't get beaten up every day for being a white kid with a Vietnamese name, between the organic dinners and this bloody lovely terrace house where we now find ourselves sat with a generous glass of South Australian red in our hands, something has gone wrong between us kiddo.

'I'm sorry you're disappointed' Tet said, and thought, but it's really not my fault that people are self-interested. On the train home she saw evidence of this: two kids snatched a doll out of one another's hands until one had the head and one had the body and both were in tears. A man pretended to be asleep so he didn't have to give up his seat for a heavily pregnant woman. She had discussed this with Barry and Julie before but he always said, 'Just proves there's not enough to go round, the workers have to fight for scraps while the boss lines his pockets.'

For Tet, her insomnia proved it. Her childhood was one long night spent in bed, unable to sleep. As each night wore on, questions grew teeth, gnawed at her. Would she kill her parents if she could sleep every night for the rest of her life? Yes, was the inevitable answer. She clenched her fists at them sleeping soundly in the next room, wishing they would suffer in her place. Sorry Mum and Dad but there's no point in fighting human nature. Which is why Tet is doing what she's doing, getting busy, getting rich.

After Tranh left, Jiang Googles sleeping and the first prediction is 'tablets.' Not so alone, she thinks. 'Image search' is like torture. Perfect couples lay entwined, eyes closed; a baby is slumped in a highchair. A woman wearing the same pyjamas as Jiang sleeps prettily on plush looking pillows, her hair spilling over them like thick black paint poured from a pot. According to the website, these pillows aid sleep. Jiang chooses the most expensive one, emails a link to Tranh at the factory. He replies instantly: *We'll talk about it tonight. Sorting out new contracts with suppliers, might have to go and visit!* He signs off with an emoticon wearing sunglasses. Smug, if an emoji can be smug. She closes her laptop, flicks on the TV and lies on the couch.

This life is beyond Jiang's wildest dreams. When she was growing up her grandparents ran a market stall at Ben Thanh market where they sold jackfruit, mango, starfruit. They were especially famous for the cumquat trees they sold for New Year. People would travel from the other side of the city, strap the trees to the back of their motorbikes, the fruit bobbing plentiful and even and sweet, the leaves shiny and green as they weaved their way home through the traffic. Her parents were educated and faithful to the party, naming their daughter after the wife of Chairman Mao. They had nice jobs teaching the official version of history. Ho Chi Minh sat above the ancestors on the altar. All her life Jiang was sure he was spying on her and gobbling up the juiciest mandarins they put out for the old people. So, they were never poor. But this; towering high above the city, the rhythms of her old life under her feet, she never imagined this. She lies down and across the city her husband orders pillows that will hopefully help her sleep in this new life she has been charmed into, swept up and thrown down in with such force that she is no longer able to dream.

Tranh throws the keys to his motorcycle down on the table, loosens his tie, pours himself two fingers of whiskey over ice. Jiang goes to kiss him.

'Did you get any sleep? Do you want a whiskey too, little cat, my princess?'

She nods. He pours.

27

'Can we talk about something important?' He hasn't loosened his tie yet and now she knows why. Still business. He moves to the couch and she follows him, more like a dog than a cat.

'My new contractors need me to sign with them. It's a big job.' He rubs his fingers together, money. 'I need to go to Australia to take cash.'

'Your father?'

Tranh shakes his head. 'More than my father could deal with, best if he doesn't know about this either. Bigger than him. I will need to go and collect, I think. Sorry, but it's necessary.'

'No no, I understand.' Jiang wonders what she will do with her time.

'I thought maybe you could manage while I'm away,' Tranh says, solving this too. 'You can definitely do it, I have no doubt.'

Jiang has no doubt that it would be much easier than her old job. Everyone told her she was lucky to get work at the big hotel but it was horrible. The tourists were so ungrateful; families from Australia wanting extra cots, cans of Coke, who complained about the size of the pool. Honeymooners from France who had sex all day and were rude to the housekeeping staff when they tried to clean, yelling *'Demain, demain.'* Groups of war veterans visited too, often for the first time since the war. They thought every woman they met was a prostitute, or they were so traumatised to be back that they pissed the bed. Enormous men formerly responsible for showering Vietnam with Agent Orange appeared at her desk, red faced; 'Well now, I'm afraid there's been an accident...' She was glad to quit when they got married.

'Sure, I'll do it.'

Tranh grins, loosens his tie and puts his feet on the coffee table, 'You ready to be rich little cat?'

Jiang sips her whiskey and smiles, hopes that will stand in for a yes.

On the day Tranh leaves, Jiang arrives at the factory to the two thousand women her husband employs streaming through the gates. They walk in the mud and the dust of the uncovered pathways to the industrial complex. They chew gum, sip tea from flasks as they walk, some smoke, chew betel and spit the red on the dirt on the path to work. Jiang stops to watch the wave of green, pink, blue and red aprons descend on the factory. This is the 'safety wear' the factory supplies. They wear masks over their mouths, some are homemade. Here a woman's mouth is covered in faded Mickey Mouse print, therein polka dots. Others wear plastic medical grade masks. Shoes made of plastic, aprons made of plastic, masks made of plastic, going to a factory to make plastics.

The three men who work directly under Tranh are already there. Jiang sits down at Tranh's desk in the small, cramped office. The bosses work on top of each other, more room for production that way. A very young woman with a heart shaped face makes everyone coffee.

'Extra milk please,' says Jiang.

The young woman nods and sweeps away. She brings it back perfectly percolated in a china cup and saucer printed with the factory logo; a unicorn. Jiang notices it is dancing with plastic products; a broom, a stool, a bowl and a container take the place of the traditional jade ball. The logo is stamped everywhere, on the wall clock, the filing cabinets. Jiang laughs.

'Is everything alright, Ma'am?'

'Sure. My husband just likes a flashy gimmick slightly more than I do.'

The girl smiles, non-committal. Probably afraid it's a trap, that she'll lose her job.

Tranh has sent her two emails; *How's it going babe?* Ten minutes later he asks, *All good?* Sunglasses emoji. Heart emoticon. Jiang tells him things are fine. She asks the men sitting in the office what her husband usually does all day. They point their lean brown fingers toward the factory floor, 'Spends time out there.'

The first thing Jiang is struck by is the noise. The crunch as women feed pellets into machines that make them into boiling plastic. Great clouds of steam and plastic dust swirl through the room, crowded with five hundred women pouring pellets, trimming excess, manufacturing red, blue, yellow, green, white, purple, orange plastic containers, all stamped with the unicorn, brightly shining under fluorescents.

The man showing Jiang round texts on his phone, checks his email, bored. He tells her the factory is environmentally friendly, recycles 10% of its plastic. The floor is covered in plastic waste, like a rainbow has fallen and shattered. Twisted pieces, blackened and charred are everywhere, all around the smell of burning. Jiang tells him to go. He is like an ironic version of a party chaperone from one of the factory tours they used to force her family and others deemed bourgeois to take. Tours meant to remind them that the heart of Vietnam lay not in the classroom, the hospital, but beat red on the factory floor. He shrugs and leaves Jiang.

Jiang, unaccompanied, watches women work. No one knows her and no one stops, no time, too risky. The tongue of the conveyor belt feeds them all different plastic shapes, all different colours; bright, hard and fast. They work so quickly their hands blur. The plastic is hot as it comes down the line but no one wears gloves, everyone sweats from the heat of the machines and each other. They have no time to wipe their faces, sweat gets caught in their face masks, some of them already wet. Women produce bowls, stools, and containers in all colours and then stack them perfectly. The bowls stand in high towers of colour, garish and beautiful, waiting for all of the hungry mouths of the world to eat from them.

If the women don't work fast enough, can't pour, pick, pack or feed fast enough Tranh will sack them. If they are older he calls them Aunty and wrings his hands as he does it. He says, 'It's not up to me, the machines set the pace, if you can't keep up, you can't work here. Sorry, but what can I do?'

All the women have a red rash. Their hands are flaking and dry at the fingernails, wet and pink on the palms. This rash grows into welts on some women's necks, in others it eats at the roots of their hair. This rash is caused by the plastics, by her husband, Jiang realises. This is her place in this production line, to make the skin of the workers fall apart and then to wander freely amongst those whose skin she is disintegrating.

A bell rings through the factory and plastics are dropped onto the conveyor belt, now still. The machines judder and clang off. Everyone moves towards the door. Jiang is swept up in the bottleneck and through the swinging doors outside. People gush like water out of a tap after a finger has been held against it. Outside it is still day and between the cinder block buildings the sky is blue, between the cinder block buildings a river flows black.

The workers begin to peel off, going down the muddy paths to one building or another. The women in front of Jiang undo their hair, ready themselves and Jiang follows them. She is met with a concrete corridor of metal doors, marked 1-9. Those beginning work are still hurrying out of the building, Jiang pushes herself against the side to let them through. A woman who has overslept rubs her eyes and runs towards the factory, where she will spend her next fifteen hours stacking piles of bowls, her green apron scrunched in her hand red with rash.

Tet arrives early to The Creativity Network where she rents a desk. Her colleagues are freelance designers, marketers and a yoga teacher who writes copy for Groupon. They stretched their criteria for Tet because they needed the extra cash. She smiles at Mark, a graphic designer who she kissed at the office Christmas Party last year. Tet got drunk on warm bubbly and ate hummus out of a plastic tub. Then she kissed Mark on the hot street below and wondered why this bunch of freelancers had clung to what was surely the worst of all office traditions.

Tet opens her laptop. She looks out at Fitzroy where she used to wait with Julie to get the tram. She would stand between her mother's legs, skirt flapping like a parachute, waiting for the tram to come and take them to the baths, the park, the pier. Now Tet looks out on a shop selling stools shaped like donuts, candelabras shaped like monkeys and scarves made from recycled plastic containers. The words *what I think is real* have been painted in fluro on the window. What do these mean, these words put next to other words?

Tet's phone rings.

'That marimba ring tone should be outlawed,' says Mark.

'Hello?'

'Yes, hello its Tranh, I'm out the front of your office.'

'I thought you'd be Vietnamese,' says Tranh with a firm handshake.

Tet laughs, 'Happens all the time.'

He is elegant in his gold wedding ring, his white shirt standing next to the gutter clogged with leaves.

'Shall we?' he asks.

Tet smooths her skirt nervously, 'Of course. Come upstairs.'

They talk and every time Tet admires his slender wrists, his calm still eyes, she shakes a peppermint from the box or taps her shoe on the edge of her chair to remind herself that this is business.

He winces on the coffee.

'Do you have any condensed milk?'

'Only soy or cows, I'm afraid.' He rips the heads off four paper cylinders of sugar and stirs it in vigorously. Tet begins to feel calmer.

Tranh makes a note to start drinking it black.

They come to a decision, a shipment of containers to start, if they prove satisfactory more to follow. They shake hands. Tranh thanks her, asks if he should go now, just a hint of a question mark. He makes no effort to get up.

'Sure, or...' Tet locks his eyes, pushes things along through the fog, 'you can work here for the day.'

'Sure,' he says, wondering why he finds the tired looking ones so sexy.

They open their identical silver laptops, their eyes meet over the cold interfaces and for Tranh it's all over now. At lunch time he goes to the toilets, uses the organic soap to ease his wedding ring off. This is a strange office with its bikes the colours children ride inside, light globes bare like the slums. What do they make here? What do they have to show for it?

Inevitably they go for drinks after work and half way through the second drink he asks 'So why *are* you called Tet?' Then he slides his hand up her leg.

'My parents are communists, supposedly. Named me after the Tet offensive.'

'I see,' laughs Tranh, a little disgusted.

'My parents are communists too, in the party.'

'Mine would be envious, I think.'

Tranh thinks of his two shrunken parents who found they could not eat their ideals and now shrug their

33

shoulders to their enterprising son and many others like him. People ask his mother day after day to look the other way. What can I do? his mother says, just as her son does.

'I doubt that,' he says, annoyed, 'In Vietnam we work and we compromise so you don't have to.'

Tet groans, 'You sound like Barry, my Marxist father.'

'I am a Marxist. The only thing Marx got wrong was the stuff about revolution.'

She kisses him then, annoyed, seduced. His tongue sneaks inside her mouth; his ashy whiskey meets her hot sweet tonic. Then he kisses her neck, lips and the scar on her chin.

The woman running late has left the door open and Jiang walks into the dorm. Her eyes adjust to the small wet towels hanging over the rails of the bunks, the unmade beds, a hairbrush clotted with hair lies on a pillow. The smell is repellent, like sleep, like sweat, perfume, joss sticks, lip gloss, hand creams, tiger balm, and a hundred other potent things people use in the tiny, snatch-able moments to keep the plastic at bay and keep something of themselves intact. There are twelve beds in this room and eleven are full. Women scramble for linen, they fling the green aprons down on the dirty floor. No one notices Jiang who watches these women she doesn't know sleep. They're curled into themselves like the unborn, scratching, snoring, breathing slow.

There is a spare bunk closest to the door. The least popular bunk for the boss.

Jiang lies down on the pillow covered in someone else's hair, smelling strongly of someone else's skin. She feels punched with exhaustion. She will be able to sleep here in a filthy dorm room but not on pillows plump with the finest goose down delivered from the United States. So, a betrayal too.

It is usually difficult for Tet to give over to sex, to give over through the brambles of the insomnia. But then it's 3am and both are drifting the way people do after they fuck. Tet feels like crying. Crying because everything has been normal and good tonight is about to fly away. He will sleep and she won't be able to fall into the place where he is. Tranh recognises that look and hopes that unlike Jiang who would leave him now to watch pop music this strange white girl with the Vietnamese name will let him comfort her.

'Come here?'

She folds into his arms. He slows his breathing. She panics that he is already asleep and has left her behind when impossibly he begins to sing, in Vietnamese, but she would recognise the Internationale anywhere. This song of her childhood now sung as a slow lullaby; 'The bullets they are rising, we'll shoot the generals on our side. So comrades come rally and the last fight let us face. The Internationale unites the human race.'

And so Tet, like Jiang, sleeps. Both of them are curled up in their place in the machine, breathing through its factories, through the guts of distribution to its luminous plastic heart.

Tet dreams of the bullets and fireworks of her namesake. In her dreams Barry chants 'Ho, Ho, Ho Chi Minh' and out of his mouth walks Julie no shoes, a photo come to life. In her dreams, there is the hiss of Barry's beer, the jingle of Julie's bracelets, the slam of the backdoor and the *ant's go marching one by one* under her skin and one hundred thousand blue containers spill across the earth. *Hurrah, hurrah!*

Jiang dreams of her Grandmother peeling pink jackfruit at the market stall sitting on a stool, on a tower

35

of plastic stools. Jiang runs in her pyjamas, in an apron through endless corridors, endless cinder block rooms numbered in stencils and her mother reaches out to tie a red kerchief around her neck and her hands turn to plastic as she sings the Internationale.

Les Petites Curies
Jane Austin

Brittany, summer 1914

My arms are strong against the tide as I swim out to sea. Waves crash carelessly over my head. I imagine myself going to rescue Maman, saving her from the insults, *down with the foreigner, husband stealer,* when they stole her letters and painted her scarlet, and she held onto us, still and dignified. The bile still rises, though I was only small at the time.

I brace my body and plough the water for one last push towards the rock. It's a scramble to get up; I find a foothold and cling onto slithery seaweed until I can haul myself, stomach first, onto the smooth stone. I sit breathless for a moment and feel the sun scorching my back. My skin is soon dry and droplets glisten on the blond hairs on my legs.

Maman is scouring Paris for X-ray equipment to save the lives of wounded soldiers, and I long to be with her. I could train as a nurse or a secretary, anything but fester in this heat. She tells me I must be brave and patient and do my maths and physics as best I can. And take care of Ève. I don't see why, I'm not her mother and Walcia is here to look after her. Those rumours about Walcia being a German spy drive me mad; people are so ignorant. They probably take us all for foreigners, so I avoid speaking Polish in public.

A prickle on my shoulders warns me my skin is burning; time to go back. I dive into the green water like a seal, smooth and sleek in her natural habitat as the tide lifts and carries me to the shore. Bring me a letter, please, Mr Postman.

Ma chère Irène,

I am glad to hear you are well occupied, but must reproach you for neglecting your little sister, who yesterday sent me a postcard full of misery. As you frequently remind me, you are old enough to take responsibility and I want you to look after her in my absence.

I'm happy to say my plans for a radiology car have taken off, thanks to the support of the Red Cross and the Union des Femmes de France. I'm now the proud owner of an automobile suitable for conversion and am well on the way to acquiring the equipment we need.

I say 'we', ma grande, because I believe together we can make ourselves useful. But first, I must safeguard the precious elements of my work, if you follow my meaning. I will send for you as soon as I can.

Fondest kisses,
Maman

I am filled with joy and remorse in equal measure.

This morning I told Ève to eat up or she'd stop growing, and fat tears gathered on her dark lashes and fell into her bowl of milk. Poor little sausage, I wish I'd comforted her.

Maman is taking her supply of radium to somewhere secure, probably far from Paris. When I was little, she'd enchant me with tales of metals that lit up like blue stars, giving out a fairy glow. Radium, her firstborn; I was so proud to go with her to Stockholm when she accepted the Nobel Prize.

'Radioactivity is a very young science,' she told me. 'It is an infant I saw being born and I have contributed to raising it with all my strength. The child has grown; it has become beautiful.'

If only she'd been talking about me. No matter, I shall learn to make myself indispensable.

Creil, November 1914

After four bone-rattling hours, we arrive in our powder blue automobile at the second army's evacuation hospital. I'm squeezed between Maman and Monsieur Ragot, an adoring student turned mechanic. I wear my nurse's uniform ready for action, irrepressible hair pinned under a triangular veil.

It took weeks to get permission to come, as the *Service de Santé* tied us up in knots. Finally, General Joffre rubber-stamped our initiative and the medical major at Creil is glad of our services.

He receives us in his office, a trim figure with a neat moustache.

'Enchanté, Madame Curie. It's a great honour.'

Maman gives a cursory nod to dispense with formalities and shakes his hand.

'We're a bit tight for space, but there's an outbuilding which I hope is suitable, Madame. I understand you are fully equipped?' He raises a bushy eyebrow.

'Yes indeed, we're quite flexible,' she replies.

'Excellent. Now let me take you to your patients.' He appears not to notice me as I trail behind, and leads the way to a densely packed ward where iron bedsteads jostle for space.

'They've been pouring in since we replaced the English, east of Soissons. Internal injuries and fractures are most common; plenty of bullets and shrapnel to get your teeth into. I hope your daughter can cope.' He accords me a cursory glance.

For a moment I doubt myself as I survey the scene. Heads wrapped in bloodied bandages, arms and legs exposed at odd angles and the unmistakable stench of gangrene; the short course in nursing taught me that. I mustn't disgrace myself or I'll bring shame on us both.

'We work as a team, Doctor, and I'd be delighted for you to observe our methods,' Maman reassures him.

'We're in your hands, Madame. Will you join me for a late lunch?'

'Thank you, but we must start at once; these poor men have waited long enough.' She stands stiffly in her black dress, a Red Cross armband on her sleeve. Today she looks more fragile than ever.

We have to transfer the equipment from the radiology car: Maman carries the delicate glass vacuum tubes and the driver wheels out the rolling rack. I take the photographic plates and the screen.

Casting an eye over the makeshift space, Maman says, 'Bring the blackouts, it's too bright in here; and we're going to need the generator.'

'*Tout de suite, Madame.*' Monsieur Ragot trots off, puppy eyed.

We're all set up, and the doctor arrives, scowling. 'This is my first experience of using an X-ray machine, Madame. I trust it won't slow things down.'

'We used it in Paris following the battle of the Marne. It undoubtedly saved lives,' Maman says tight-lipped.

'J'espère bien,' he replies with a snort of acknowledgement.

I feel clumsy in my protective apron, goggles and gloves, and watch as the first patient is wheeled in. Orderlies transfer the stretcher to our portable table. A sheet covers the boy's lower body; his dark eyes are full of fear. The doctor gives a nod and I realise I must pull back the sheet.

There's a gaping wound to the inner thigh. Maman looks on impassively and I look away from the gory mess.

'Let's take a look,' says the doctor, from behind his surgical mask.

Maman positions the glass vacuum tube under the table and lowers the screen over the wound. 'What's your name?' she asks.

'Tardy, Émile Tardy.' He sounds even younger than he looks.

'This won't hurt, Émile. We're going to examine your wound by looking at a photograph.' She signals for me to turn on the power.

An image emerges showing a dark shadow, a hard-edged object lodged in flesh. Once the doctor has observed it, I turn off the beam to minimise exposure.

'It's not too deep; a few drops of this and we'll have it out in no time,' he says, applying anesthetic to the area.

The boy's shoulders tense.

We show the image intermittently, seconds at a time, moving the screen back and forth to enable the doctor to work. He probes the wound with his pincers, glances at the image, returns to his task and looks up again, until he sees the points of the pincers holding the foreign body. He withdraws the instrument and the boy cries out, tears streaming down his face.

It's over. A bloody mess of tissue and shrapnel lies in a kidney dish.

Shaking, pull off gloves and goggles and brush sweat from my face with the back of my hand, ashamed.

Maman strokes the boy's forehead and says gently, 'You're very brave, Émile.'

I'm sure she used to do the same for us, though I have no recollection of it; all I remember is Papa and Maman spending every spare moment at the laboratory.

'Not bad for a novice?' says the doctor, lifting his mask to reveal a broad smile and crooked teeth.

'Fine work,' says Maman, and winks at me.

My heart flutters with joy to be fighting this war at her side, her daughter and trusted assistant.

Two orderlies transfer the boy onto a trolley and wheel him out; I feel his pain as they trundle him across the cobbles. 'Will they sew him up?' I want to know, as the doors bang closed.

'A nurse will see to it; he'll be good as new by tomorrow,' the doctor says heartily.

Maman takes notes and shows me her method. 'Take today for example: *Tardy, Émile, Fourteenth chasseurs, pain in the leg, shell fragment in the right thigh removed; depth 10cm.* You can do the next one.'

The familiar routines of science are a comfort, distancing me from the suffering. We work for countless days, as the wounded are ferried from the Front. I soon learn my first experience was exceptional, as most injuries are too deep to operate on the spot. I take X-ray shots from different angles and develop plates for use during surgery. I've learned how to locate a projectile using a protractor and simple geometry. You'd think it was magic, to see the astonishment on the doctor's face.

This evening I walk with Maman, arm in arm, to our quarters on the outskirts of the hospital grounds. My head and feet ache. We don't bother to say how tired we feel.

Heavy gunfire pounds in the distance and I think of cousin Maurice, who wears irony like a second skin: 'I am going back into the trenches to serve breakfast as usual to Messieurs Boches. They are used to it. This morning they don't respond, which makes the job easier, because it has become a job, this war that never ends.'

Since working at the hospital, my feelings about the war have altered. At first, I saw it as a challenge to solve medical problems using modern science. Now I feel weighed down by its relentless power to maim and destroy. So many wounded, patched up, and sent back to be broken again.

'Tell me, Maman, is it possible to be a *patriote* and hate the war?'

'Of course, my dear. It's the only intelligent response in these times of slaughter.'

Her directness surprises me; she's so passionate about being French. We walk on in silence awhile.

'There's so much more to be done, Irène, dear. I want to equip a fleet of radiology cars and train young women as operators. You'd be an excellent teacher, if you have the stamina to continue.'

I choke back a sob; it's all I've ever wanted, to work for her.

She pats my hand. 'Forgive me, I know I can be hard on you. I forget you're only seventeen.'

'I'll never leave you, Maman,' I blurt out, brushing away tears.

I hear her sigh. 'My life's work has made me sick; but you know that. You are well able to continue my research, Irène. I wonder if you shall.'

'You're worn out, Maman, you mustn't speak like this.' I tighten my grip on her sleeve.

'Ève will need you; such a sensitive soul, pouring out her heart at the piano. You and I are more cerebral.'

I flinch. Don't I have feelings too? It's a flesh wound, but it stings. I fumble for the key of the cottage. Once inside, I go to the oil lamp and hold a match to the wick.

Maman busies herself at the grate. 'We've been called to the Front, thanks to the Major's recommendation. We'll have patients on the table directly from the battlefield, before suppuration has time to develop.' Straightening herself, her steady grey eyes meet mine. 'It's just what we've been waiting for, *non*?'

I feel the tiredness melt away; I may even be happy.

'Where shall we sleep?' I ask, catching her mood.

She gives a rare smile. 'In a tent, of course; where else?'

For a moment I'm a child again, at the start of a great adventure.

References:
Madame Curie, by Eve Curie, Heinemann
The Great Nobel Prizes, The Curie Family, by Maurice Goldsmith, Heron Books
Marie and Pierre Curie, by John E. Senior, Sutton Publishing
Marie Curie, by Robert Reid, The Quality Book Club and the Scientific Book Club
Marie Curie, A Life, by Susan Quinn, Heinemann

Whatever Happened To Sarah-Jayne
Kathryn Lund

One Tile

Orson's desk was in Orson's office. Orson's office consisted of:

Orson's computer.

Orson's un-killable pot plant.

Orson's posture-support execu-chair.

Orson's walls.

There were eight and three quarter blue worn carpet tiles, one door, one window, one view of the road. And one view of the sign for Purified Petra-Chemico Research Appliances Break-Out Division Co.

Orson was not sure what Purified Petra-Chemico Research Appliances Break-Out Division Co. did but he did it. For fifteen years now, at his desk with the unkillable pot plant and the carpet tiles. He was doing it then, as he did what everyone does at work, which is play on Facebook and Google a little light porn.

Then it happened.

Orson's office—neat, tidy, smudged with a dirty film of traffic from the motorway below, went away. A white, painfully empty corridor appeared in its place. Orson's desk was in the middle of it. Orson was at the desk.

That was all, absolutely nothing else happened to Orson.

It was after a pause, when perhaps moved by some change in the quality of light, or maybe in the silence, Orson looked up. He saw the corridor, saw the long white walls, the outlines of doors. He had a thought, which was different than the one you or I might have in that moment. It was finally, *finally*.

Then Orson did what he always did whenever anything happened. He continued sitting, at his desk. Time might have passed, or not. People may have come and gone and moved and existed, banged into his office shouting

'Hey, Orson'

—or not. Orson did not know. Orson simply continued to sit.

Then something like interest began to show on his round, slackened face. He slid back the posture-support execu-chair. You could hear the sound of it, scratching on the veneer of the silence.

Nothing.

Orson went around the desk. He started a neat, but cautious, little walk into the white space beyond. A corridor, tiles, many doors on either side, stretching on in a big yawn of shape. Orson walked down it. Nothing but walking and doors.

Orson stopped. Looked at a door. It had a sign. The sign read

The Cloakroom.

Orson stood, thought for a moment. There was something about this. This felt…

…familiar. Like he had opened one door in his head to find another. A door he knew, though then it was bigger, or he was smaller. Yes, that's right. He was small, he would have to reach right up to touch the handle, strain to try and spell out the letters on the sign:

C---L----O----A----/ —

It was over. Orson was sitting at Orson's desk. Orson's desk was in Orson's office. Orson's office closed in with Orson's un‑killable pot plant, Orson's posture-support execu-chair, eight and three quarter blue worn carpet tiles, one door, one window, one view of the road.

The silence changed again around him, a noisy silence of background that dared him to say it had ever gone away. No-one came in, or out. No-one said

'Hey, Orson'

So Orson did what he always did. He sat at his desk.

He sat there.

Two Tiles

Orson's drive to Purified Petra-Chemico Research Appliances Break-Out Division Co. was forty-four and a half minutes. Orson drove it, every day, for one week.

He made the 8.55 coffee with Janette from People Responses. He watched the taut, firm arch of her denier strain up off the floor to reach the sugar caddy. He carried the tray for her.

On Thursday, The Laundress of Leominster went offline. On Friday he spread his hands beneath the table of conference room Alpha Blue and counted the grains of the wood. On the projector the new Five Tier Ethics and Environment for Working Contract blurred on screen. The slide changed.

It happened again.

There on the screen, made up of light filters, speckled with dust nodes, Orson could see a room. The room consisted of:

table in country-style pine,

AGA

chintz curtains,

semi-fitted, eclectic units,

neat, untidy Things.

Orson looked at it, confused, unable to work out how this fitted into the new Five Tier Ethics and Environment for Working Contract.

On the units, on screen, a cat unfolded. Orson watched the cat. The cat ignored Orson. Still unfolding, it walked; tabby and rather fat. Fell off the edge of the light-picture, landed, rather affronted, in conference room Alpha Blue.

Absolutely nothing happened. No one noticed. No one said, 'Hey Orson, there's this cat'

This time Orson had exactly the same thought as you or I, which was *insanity*. The cat did what all cats would. Somehow look to Orson like falling was intentional, that landing out of projector screens was *dull*. It rolled on the carpet and stretched.

Orson watched the cat. Watched the saunter over, the rubbing of Orson's ankle, the twist around Orson's leg. How it somehow communicated to him, Orson, that all things considered—the universe weighed up, all other options put aside—it was for that moment, Orson's cat. The light-room glowed on screen.

Orson looked at the room, got up.

The cat got up.

Orson walked towards the light-room. The cat walked towards the light-room.

It was in front of him—AGA, chintz curtains, semi-fitted, eclectic Things—all contained inside the plastic of the frame. He had no idea what to do. Finally, the impatient cat head butting his shin, Orson began to heave one leg over the side, a man climbing over the edge of a large paddling pool.

He was in. He was there.

It smelled of them. Of scrubbed pine, kitchen table, chintz curtains, eclectic units, AGA, things on the fridge, of hundreds and thousands of days eaten away on those chairs. It could have been any time outside those windows. Orson had the feeling of still, cut-off February mornings of overnight snow. He had the stretched timeless breath of long summer afternoons when you come in from the sun and felt the cool of shaded rooms. It was all in here.

Orson was in here too. But differently. The weight had gone, here was a lighter Orson. Here was Orson without the polyester mix stretched shirt and in-packet matching tie. Here was Orson without carelessness wrapped round his gut. He looked up. Looked around, curious about what this Orson would see. It wasn't familiar and yet...

...it was. There was something in here. Something under those hand drawn pictures on the fridge, something under the cat that plumped it up like an invisible cushion as it lounged, tail over the AGA rail. Something under this whole room that teased Orson like a finger through his memory, poking, twisting.

Finding a thread. Marijuana, bad lighting, unwashed skin, awful grunge track played over and over. Blue bandana bleeding into her skin at Glastonbury. All bleeding into one, here. Was she somewhere, here? Orson ran towards the stripped wood door.

His feet were lighter. Dried oranges with cloves hung on the back. Bags for life. Elephants on bell-strung strings. He opened the door.

Impossibly white blinding corridor. Doors leading off on either side. Light, quiet, empty of anyone but Orson.

Orson looked at the door. It had a sign. The sign was a name. Orson knew what it was before he read it. There was only one name it could be. The name read:

Sarah-Jayne.

Three Tiles

Orson's drive to Purified Petra-Chemico Research Appliances Break-Out Division Co. was forty-four and a half minutes. He travelled it, every day, he watched the 10 denier 8.55 stretch. He carried the tray, he logged on. He got through Monday, Tuesday, Wednesday. Thursday he walked four times round the waiting room belonging to Trish and sat in her chair.

Trish featured with regularity in the life of Orson, though he didn't count times. He admitted her usefulness. It was some time after all since he had paced the eight and three-quarter blue square carpet tiles which made up his coveted office at Purified Petra-Chemico Research Appliances Break-Out Division Co. He had stopped with the lights.

But sat in the chair Orson ran out the following dialogue.

Trish: can you tell me what it looks like in your head, this feeling?
I, Orson: Like a sort of corridor
Trish: A corridor? Can you tell me about the corridor, or what you are feeling when you think about the corridor?
I, Orson: It's sort of like I've got to walk down it, and there are doors.
Trish: (listens)
I, Orson: The doors have things written on them.
Trish: What things?
I, Orson: ...things.
Trish: Are these 'things' like the compulsions we've been working on?
I, Orson: ...maybe... I don't know... I think I have to go through them, I have to go up and down the corridor, I have to check.
Trish: Why do you have to do that Orson?

I, Orson: I don't know.

Trish: You're very safe here Orson you know there are no wrong thoughts.

I, Orson: I know.

(a pause)

Trish: You're inside your head, checking things. What have we learned so far about why we do this?

I, Orson: It's about fight or flight.

Trish:(listens)

I, Orson: (giving in) I know I can't control the universe, I know, it's patterns in my head.

Trish: Do you think that this new pattern, your corridor, is helpful Orson?

I, Orson: (lying) No, I know it's not.

Trish:That's good, Orson. Do you think that you would like to work on your new corridor?

I, Orson: (lying) I can give it a go.

Trish: OK then, you're in your corridor. Everything is telling you must walk down the corridor, is that right?

I, Orson: Yes.

Trish: Why?

I, Orson: (silent)

Trish: You know how this works, Orson, it's all connected to something. What are you trying to do by walking down the corridor?

I, Orson: I'm–(but how can I, Orson, tell her, when she doesn't understand. About the realness of The Cloakroom, what I told Sarah-Jayne) ...I'm...

Orson stopped. Whatever he practised, Orson couldn't explain the corridor was, well,—real. Physical. Not a thing inside his head whilst the world went on outside. Orson saw it. Orson *felt* it. Saw it as he saw his Managers-Must–Have-Motivators Top-Tips Calendar.

Orson stood up, walked four times round again and left. It was seventeen and one quarter minutes back to his Office. Orson clicked the radio all the way back until he cut off the engine and parked.

Four Tiles, Five

Orson's drive home from Purified Petra-Chemico Research Appliances Break-Out Division Co. was forty-four and a half minutes. He drove to his flat, reversed. Drove twenty seven minutes and ten seconds back down the motorway. Parked on the multi-storey in the fifth slot from the end. Remained calm.

It was now Friday. In the foyer Orson located the layout map, signed in, counted the steps up to his wanted floor. He counted three double flights of ten steps each. This helped him for a while and he hardly had to sit at a desk for long, not really long at all.

The library went on, quietly around him. Absolutely no one paid attention to him. He felt the quietness, and the long blank still of the place. He breathed it in and felt his calm.

Then Orson began. There was lots of books. Orson looked at most of them. He pulled them neatly off the shelves with his rather over-large fingers. He pushed them back on. Off and on off and on. This went some time. Only the quickening scrape of book spines half-dragged from shelves, only the sweat clogging between his fingers, only these outwardly spoke of his growing desperation, but it was there.

His breath began to shorten, the slam, slam of books began to quicken to a running stampede along the close packed shelves. Orson felt that horrible slosh inside him as the need to *finish* and the need to *do* battled it out in his stomach grounds.

It happened again.

A librarian appeared. Orson knew it was a librarian because it looked like one. It wore a bow tie and tweed. The librarian said:

—*Looking for something?*

Orson stood there, looking at the librarian.

—*Something specific, for something on your mind?*

There was something about that, the way the librarian said it. Like it could read—read the things that wrote across the blank walls of Orson's head. Things like:

Sarah Jayne and the blue bandana / the Cloakroom and what had happened there.

Things like how he, Orson, should never have told her. How he should have let it all blow away into pot smoke and grass.

The librarian looked at Orson. Orson looked backed.

—*This one, I think,* said the librarian.

It was a sort of dark pinkish-red. Textured cover. The sort that ruffles goose-bumps if brushed the wrong way. Small. Heavy. On its back. No blurb. Just the cover and on the cover, picked out in blue paint, was the name that Orson knew.

Orson tried to open the book. He could not. Orson tried to shake the book, desperate to see its contents. He could not. It stayed closed, silent, in his hands. He read the front again:

This is the book of Sarah-Jayne.

Orson ran. He didn't count stairs. He didn't touch-wood desk-chairs or check doors as he passed.

He ran.

Out of breath. Not a fit man. At the point of collapsing, hanging onto stairs. Which is when the librarian said:

—*Looking for something? Something on your mind perhaps?*

The librarian reached out his hands, gave back This is the Book of Sarah-Jayne. Orson looked up.

A white, painfully empty corridor appeared in front of Orson. Orson's desk was in the middle of it. Orson was leaning on the desk. A sort of pinkish-red door with a blue coloured plaque glowed to the side.

The librarian coughed, politely. Orson managed— nothing. He was out of breath.

—*When you're ready,* said the librarian.

—*Ready? Ready for what?*

—*You tell me.*

The librarian perched on Orson's desk. Orson's Managers-Must-Have-Motivators-Top-Tips-Calendar toppled at the touch of tweed backside. Orson looked around, confused.

—*Honestly Orson, haven't you worked it all out yet? Still, only to be expected. I mean look at you. You're carrying it around like a gutful of slob.*

The librarian smiled at Orson. The corridor stretched. Orson felt the face above him grow as empty as the corridor and as strange. Nothing happened. The stretch of the corridor continued, long and pulled out like a spine on a rack. Orson felt what you or I would in those long, heavy weights that passed for seconds, which was uncomfortable. Increasingly skin-pricked and cold, sweat itching in his toes.

Orson turned away and walked towards the pinkish-red door. Stopped. Looked at the door, looked back at the librarian who lounged now on the desk, body locked in a cheerful wave.

Turned again, back to the door. Tried to open the door. Could not.

Shook the door, desperate to see its contents. Could not.

Banged on the door, urgent, rattling the handle, heaving his body against its bulk. Could not get through, could only feel it, feel it all in there—sudden mornings of silent snow, summer swallowed shade, marijuana smoke grown to perfumes, grunge track playing over and over through the background of their days. In there, somewhere, he knew it, *Sarah-Jayne.*

Orson pounded the door.

—*Honestly Orson, haven't you worked it all out yet? haven't you?*

It was over.

The wailing tear of the alarm pulled something apart inside him, starting at his bladder, finishing at his lungs. There were staircases—three flights of them exploding like a logic puzzle above his head—and people. If they knew his name, they would have been saying, 'Hey, Orson.'

They were settling for other words, shouting.

There was the fire-door bar, rattling in Orson's hand.

Orson did what anyone would do now. Orson lost his calm.

Six, Seven, Eight Tiles

In the following week, these are the things that Orson did:

Orson sat at Orson's desk.

Orson counted Orson's things.

Orson checked the bad places in his head.

Orson drew the patterns that protected

Orson counted squares, there were eight and three-quarters of them plus one door and one window and forty four and a half minutes to and from this place.

Orson had 8.55 which was People Responses and 9.05 which was Carrying The Tray.

Orson had watching, unstinted by credit card limits, the Laundress of Leominster steam her way through topless sheets and all was well with her, fine with her—she was online throughout the week.

Orson didn't need a change in the quality of the silence to tell him. It had happened. A white, painfully empty elsewhere, with Orson's desk in the middle of it, Orson standing at the desk.

Enduring, in agony, at his desk.

—*You're an idiot, Orse.*

Sarah-Jayne. There, in front of him. Cross-legged in tweed and a bow tie, grinning as cream-smug as a cat. Pot smoke curled from her fingers. The smell of unwashed summer, promise, sex. The smell of Sarah-Jayne.

Orson looked up at her. This is the Book of Sarah-Jayne lay open across her thighs. She thumbed through, indifferent.

—*Bit un-original isn't it—is this where you shove me Orse? I mean, please. Can you say obvious?*

The thing that might be Sarah-Jayne took a deep drag, looked at him, rolled her baked little eyes. Such boredom; it had poured out of her, in the end, like a cat with old fish.

—*Poor stupid you. I mean, do you really think you can get there this way? You really think that's the way back?*

Her laugh, her horrid little laugh, the way she had done it in the end.

—You don't control the universe you know.

That laugh again, her long hair rolling.

—Man, that's deep, I may be cooked.

The corridor roared up in front of Orson. There was the throbbing door of pinkish-red. Dried oranges with cloves were hung on the back, bags for life. Elephants on bell–strung strings. Orson was sure of it. Orson was *sure*.

—No, not there—you're an idiot, Orse!

That wasn't Sarah-Jayne. Some likeness of Sarah-Jayne only. Some Sarah-Jayne-Thing he didn't have to listen to. He ran to the door, pulled on the door, opened the door. It *opened* this time.

—No, Orse!

Orson entered through the door.

The kitchen was in front of Orson. This was his house, his kitchen. Orson believed in it. Orson had always believed, known it existed somewhere. Orson had found it, it was here.

All those times he had counted patterns in his head, all those times he had paced the eight and three-quarter blue squares of the coveted office of Purified Petra-Chemico Research Appliances Break-Out Division Co., he had done it to save this. To undo what he had done in the cloak room—and how he had told it to Sarah-Jayne.

He looked around him. On the table a book, light blue cover. Title rough cut, charred out as though by a burn. Shut, on its front. Orson nudged over to it. Read:

This is The Book of Sarah-Jayne / What Became of a Boy Called Orson.

Orson stopped, looked at the book. Felt—uncertain. The uncertainty grew from his bladder, finished at his lungs.

Orson stood, doing nothing. In his kitchen, getting more and more breathless, feeling strange. Sweat clogged between his fingers, dripped. The horrible feeling sloshed inside him, a wet blackness that found a grip, then started to stick.

Nothing, nothing, in long, stretching time.

He poked, tentatively, at the book. Pulled at the cover of the book. Opened the book.

Water rushed out like a gush of rain across a muddy field. Dirty, brown, stinking of stagnant pits, of clogged-up days. It ran and ran. It ran all over Orson. It spewed out like a flatulent gut.

Ran, ran, more water than a book could contain, than a gut or lungs or a body could contain if you pressed it down to its sixty-five percent water and threw it over Orson. Rotten, chocked and dirty, running eventually to rivulets down his legs.

It stopped, leaving only wetness and a blue bandana. Soaking, covered in mud. Orson could see its colours bleeding out. He reached like a man up to elbows down some drain, picked it up, feeling it like he had that last time. He could remember—the mud and Sarah-Jayne.

I mean, do you really think you can get there this way? You really think that's the way back?

Different voice this time, younger, sweeter. Then that last cry, urgent and without shame—

—*No, you're an idiot, Orse!*

Orson tried to hold on. Onto the scrubbed table, tea-towel cat, art-work fridge, sun-snow seasons, unwashed memories, blue bandana twisted round his hand. But it was no good. Orson knew. Orson understood.

Orson had got it wrong. He sat at the table. He waited it out.

It was over.

Around him Purified Petra-Chemico Research Appliances Break-Out Division Co. materialised. Orson's desk, Orson's office, Orson's unkillable pot plant, Orson's posture-support execu-chair, eight and three quarter blue worn carpet tiles, one door, one window, one view of the road. One screen. The screen blinked.

Blinked.

Orson's hands were empty. Orson's gut pushed on the confines of his roll-back execu-chair arms. From below the smudge of dirty traffic noise wiped itself across the Room. Orson sat, watching it grow.

Orson sat, waited it out. One screen, one desk, one view of the road, one traffic smudge, he watched it grow. He had an unkillable plant and he watched noise grow. At 5.03 he drove the forty-four and a half minutes home.

Absolutely nothing happened to Orson. Nothing happened to him at all.

Three Quarter Tiles, the room was whole.

Eclipsed
Kate Mitchell

It's our first night on board so we dress for the occasion: me in my best bib and tucker, and Amanda wearing her plungiest neckline with the white gold pendant I bought her for Christmas. We've barely sat down to dinner when I hear, 'I don't believe it!' which makes me think of that character on TV, but the chap bouncing towards us looks too young to remember the sitcom. He stops in front of our table and smiles at Amanda. When she doesn't speak I look at her and see she's staring down at the table. The skin on her neck is a mottled pink. Perhaps she's seasick; but we've barely left Newcastle and the North Sea is like a millpond.

Thinking this must be an acquaintance of hers, I stand up and hold out my hand. He grabs at it with a sort of damp, two fingered slide, saying, 'Felix, you must be Dan,' while his eyes slip over me and back to Amanda. He says, 'Fiona, look who it is,' and I notice a young lady has joined him. She smiles politely, with a little shake of her head. 'It's Amanda,' he says, 'You remember—'

She clearly doesn't but she's polite enough to say, 'Of course, how do you do?' Amanda ignores Fiona's outstretched hand. To make up for my wife's unaccountable rudeness, I take Fiona's hand and squeeze it warmly, and introduce myself. She's a pretty thing, tall and slim, looking as though she's poured herself into that black sheath of a dress. I check whether Amanda has noticed the effect this girl is having on me; she generally does and we'd have a chuckle about it, later. But Amanda looks as though she's about to faint.

Without invitation, this Felix seats himself opposite Amanda, babbling on about 'amazing coincidence,' and laughing. He seems a bit over-excited but I'm used to that. I'm guessing by his age that he's been in the trainee programme at Amanda's practice. The young ones do tend to go doe-eyed around her. She's not only renowned as an expert in family law, but, if I say it myself, she's sophisticated and has a quick wit that leaves most barristers looking as stale as last year's bread.

Fiona seems a little non-plussed, so I wave her into the seat opposite me and in a few seconds the waiter arrives with the wine list. Felix glances at it and with the precision of someone who's recently learned to pronounce it, orders a sauvignon blanc. When I order the house wine, he says, 'Should that be boat wine?' and laughs again, a high-pitched giggle that sounds rather camp.

I make small talk with Fiona, who seems a delightful young lady. He's taking no notice of the poor girl. The ship's photographer pauses beside the table and I'm waving him away when Felix says he'd like a picture. He leans towards Amanda and puts his hand over hers and the camera has flashed before she pulls it away and drops it on her lap.

I ask Fiona if she's cruised before. They don't look the cruising type. They must be the only people under fifty, and part of a minority that doesn't need mobility aids to get in and out of their cabins.

'This is our first time,' she says. 'Felix organised it at the last minute as a surprise. I never knew he was so keen on eclipses, but he's very excited.' So I see.

The wine arrives and he makes a show of the tasting. It's *table d'hôte* and the waiter brings our starter, shrimp cocktail. Amanda pokes at hers so I whisper to ask if she's okay, and she snaps, 'Stop fussing'.

I ask Felix, 'How do you know my wife?'

'You mean she's never mentioned me?' he sounds surprised.

'Can't say she has. Workwise, is it?'

Amanda pipes up, 'That's right. Felix was one of my trainees last year.' As I thought.

During the main course, which is a very splendid quail stuffed with black pudding, and an almond mash, I gather from Fiona that they live in Manchester, work in city centre law practices, and plan to move out to one of the villages, maybe Uppermill. This is where we live, I tell her; it's very pleasant and an easy commute. We chat a bit about property and it turns out they're interested in a house in the very next street.

She reminds me a lot of Amanda; assured and confident with a spark about her; and the same way of swinging her dark brown bob, so that her eyes are screened intermittently when she's talking. It's coy and quite sexy. He is something of a dullard by contrast; not much to say for himself, laughing too much and drinking rather fast. Amanda only joins in the conversation with a yes or no every now and again. She excuses herself before dessert, saying she's not feeling too well and is off to her cabin. It's a suite, actually, but she probably thinks that might sound like showing off.

I don't think she sleeps very well. At various times through the night I hear her padding about. She must be over-exhausted, I think. It's been a particularly busy time for her this last year, with more out-of-town cases, up and down to London at least twice a week. Her phone never stops with emails and messages, and I've known her to work on court papers through the night sometimes. This cruise is a rare holiday. I wish she'd join me in retirement—we talked about travelling, not just taking holidays but hiring a Winnebago maybe, touring the States—but Amanda says she's not ready to slow down. She is ten years younger than me, probably at the peak of her profession. When I see youngsters like this

Felix acting all puppy-like around her, I get a glimpse of the kudos she must find in her work so it's perhaps not surprising that she wants to carry on.

In the morning, she looks tired, and when Felix jumps up from a table in the breakfast buffet and calls us to join him, I feel her sag beside me.

'We can use the other restaurant,' I suggest, but she sighs, 'Too late now,' and joins the young people. Fiona looks a little put out. Maybe she expected a romantic getaway and finds herself lumbered with the old folk. I can't say I blame her. This old folk would rather not get in the way of the young romantics. Not that this Felix seems to pay much attention to his lady. Maybe that's what's cheesing her off.

Today is spent at sea. Amanda doesn't want to come to the astronomy lecture, to find out about the eclipse; she prefers to stay in the suite and read. Afterwards, I join a Bridge Tour, which is very interesting indeed. This Captain is definitely a man to trust with your life in a storm. He shows us the instruments and tells us all about how he changed direction during the night to minimise the swell and the roll. A lady asks how long it would take to rescue someone who fell overboard. Fifteen minutes, apparently, to lower the boat and bring it round, recover the person and bring them back on board. Much longer in poor weather, the Captain says, and in some conditions it can be very difficult indeed, if not impossible. In the dark, for example, or when the alarm is not raised promptly.

Amanda stays in our suite, resting until dinner time, and we are barely through the door of the restaurant when Felix is behind us. Fiona's smile may be starting to get a bit thin.

During dinner, I say, casually, 'One of the best things about this cruise company is that they have open seating,' and when he looks quizzically at me, I explain, 'Often on cruises, you have an allocated place for meals, but here, we can sit where we like, so we meet different people. It's part of the fun of it.'

I think Fiona understands me, for after dinner she says to him, 'Let's go into the bar, and leave Amanda and Dan in peace.'

To circumvent any further discussion, I put my hand under Amanda's elbow and say, 'We'll see you later, then.' His eyes scorch my back until we are through the swing door.

We sit in the lounge, listening to the concert. At one point Amanda's phone bleeps and when she takes it out of her bag and looks at it, I ask, 'One of the boys?' and she shakes her head, saying, 'The office. Just a quick query.'

Irritated, I say, 'You'd think the office could allow you a bit of a break.'

She says, 'I'm going on deck for some air.'

'If you hang on, I'll get our coats', but she's out of the door before the words are out of my mouth. I sit through the rest of the concert, half listening to the Filipino singer strangling songs such as 'Tie a Little Ribbon Round the Yellow Tree', thinking about how off Amanda seems. Slowly I start to think it may be me, me and her, something I've done, or not done, but I can't work out what. Afterwards, I look out on the promenade deck, and make out some figures close together in the dark, but there's no sign of Amanda. She isn't back at the suite, either, and while I'm waiting I nod off.

When I hear her moving about, I look at my watch and say, 'It's two in the morning'.

'I picked up some emails,' she says. 'The Ulceby case. It needed a response before court sits in the morning. There's a better signal in the lounge.'

She's worn out and tetchy so I say nothing, but I make a mental note to have a word with Colin, her partner and my squash buddy. When I next check my watch, it's half past seven in the morning and she isn't there. I dress quickly and search the dining room and the lounges, but there's no sign of her. Fiona is eating breakfast alone. Back at the suite, Amanda is in the shower. I wonder whether I missed her, earlier, but I think not.

From our balcony we watch the ship coming into the dock at Torshavn. Amanda suggests taking a walk, independently, rather than going on the tour we've booked. The tour coach passes us as we walk into town, and I see her number one fan staring out of the window, looking somewhat disconsolate. I give him a little wave. The town is crowded, on account of this being one of the two best places in the world to see the eclipse. At the Tourist Information Centre we find a map and walk through a delightful little plantation, past the statues in the garden at the art gallery, and up to the Nordic House where they have a rather tasty Eclipse Beer on sale.

On our way back, we stand at the viewpoint, a memorial to those lost at sea during World War Two. Beyond the turf-topped roofs of Torshavn, our ship is moored in the narrow harbour, crammed alongside several other eclipse-seeking cruise ships. Watching the clouds speeding across the huge horizon, I feel a sense of largeness, of anything being possible.

'I've something to tell you,' Amanda says. I remember my reflections of last night, and my world tilts. She puts my hand in hers and strokes the backs of my fingers with her thumb, and tells me that she had a 'bit of a fling' with Felix. 'Bit of a fling' is how she puts it. Nothing to worry about, then. We've each had our moments; it's separate to our life together, that side of things; both of us knowing but not talking about it, and it's made us stronger, if anything. So why do I feel suddenly hollow, as though I have lost my centre, my core? It's because

Amanda is telling me about it, which means that this was different. Important.

'Serious?' I ask.

She shrugs. 'It wasn't. A couple of dinners, after late nights preparing for court.' She pauses. 'And… when we were in London.'

I see at once. 'So these "out of town" cases. "Staying in London"? You were with him?' She doesn't answer, so I know. 'So it is serious?' Her eyes are wet. I think it's because she's trying to tell me that we are over. I turn away from her, try to focus back on the skyline but it seems to be moving. 'The so-called London cases have been running for—what? Seven, eight months? And now, he's joined you on holiday? To do what, exactly? And what's his girlfriend doing? If she is his girlfriend. Perhaps she's a cover for him so he can carry on with you —a decoy—'

'Of course she's his girlfriend.'

'So you're both making a fool of her, too?'

'Dan, you're being ridiculous now.'

'Me being ridiculous? Have you any idea how ridiculous it is, for a woman in her fifties to be infatuated with a boy the same age as her own son?'

Squealing and giggling from the footpath below quiets us while a group of children makes their way past, pushing and shoving one another.

'I didn't know he was coming on the trip,' she says.

'And now he has? What do you intend to do?'

'It's over. I told him. It was just a fling—stupid, I know, but I was flattered—'

'When did you tell him?'

'Last month. Last week.' I realise she is crying. Amanda doesn't cry. 'Last night. Again, and again—'

'What are you saying? That he won't take no for an answer?'

'Precisely that. He——I don't know how to say this——it makes me feel so stupid, but I think he's stalking me. He's, he's everywhere I go——'

There's a bench on the pathway, beside a duck pond. Here, she tells me about all the times she's tried to tell him it's over, and how he keeps appearing, wherever she is. Even on the street outside our home, for goodness' sake, telling her he's looking at houses in the area. Coming on this trip is his way of forcing the issue; apparently he's planning to tell me tonight. It comes to me that what is happening to Amanda could so easily have happened to me; 'bunny boilers' I think they call these people.

We head down the hill, to the harbour, and are back on the ship, watching from our balcony when the coach returns from the tour. Within the queue of passengers snaking from the bus, along the dockside, and up the gangway, Felix is looking around, then up, and we move back to stay out of sight. We go in to dinner late and walk past the table where Felix sits, waving, deliberately taking the only two spare seats at a table further along. Afterwards, we order wine from room service and carry on talking, until late into the night.

Exhausted, we are woken by the ping-pong of the speaker followed by the Captain's voice: 'Ladies and gentlemen, as you know, the only two landfalls where the eclipse will be visible today will be Faro Islands and Spitzbergen. The only place where there will be totality will be on the track of the eclipse across the North Atlantic. During the night I have positioned the ship so we are now on this track. Please be aware that it is foggy and whilst we are hoping that this will clear sufficiently for you to have a view, it cannot be guaranteed.'

The cabin steward brings us breakfast, and we phone the boys and manage to get hold of Drew although it's a dodgy signal by satellite. Drew, of course, is cock-a-hoop that from where he lives, in Oxfordshire, the day is mild and cloudless, perfect for a ninety-five percent eclipse. He also tells us that the aurora borealis was visible over much of northern England last night, so all in all he doesn't quite understand why we've gone to the expense of this trip. We share a chuckle with him. I don't of course tell him that if we can get his mum back to normal, this trip will have been worth every penny. It's not what I came here for, but it's certainly what I need to do before I go home.

Just before ten, we're on the little side deck, a fairly quiet spot beneath the main promenade deck, wrapped warmly against the wind, listening to the professor of astronomy narrating events over the loudspeaker. Every few minutes the cloud clears to give us a tantalizing glimpse of the sun as it moves towards eclipse. It's getting darker and colder by the second. The door behind us slams and I look around to see Felix emerging. In his wake, Fiona, looking somewhat put out. I think she's complaining about being on this deck, for I hear her say, '——had a perfectly good view.' He more or less knocks me out of the way to stand between us. Amanda looks at him and then round him, raising her eyebrows at me.

I say, very quietly, 'One chance, to leave my wife alone.'

He looks at me with a sneer. 'Or else?' All pretence of friendliness has been dropped.

I say, 'She's not interested.'

'Oh, you think?' He moves his lips to my ear and whispers, 'She and I have done things ——you could never know——'

I shouldn't stoop to his one-upmanship game but I can't help it. 'What I know for sure, sonny, is that of all the little dalliances my wife has had, the only thing that marks you out is that you're the most recent.'

He sniggers and says, 'What we have is special.'

'No,' I say, 'Amanda and me, that's what is special.' Amanda has moved along and is now at the corner of the deck, where a length of open railing, a metre or so, meets the side of the boat. She is watching the waves hitting the boat directly below.

There's a whoop from the main deck above, a crackle from the loudspeaker, and the astrologer tells us that the clouds have cleared in time for total eclipse in just a few seconds.

Felix gets hold of Amanda's arm, shakes it, says, 'Tell him.'

I look around at the sound of a sob and there's Fiona, mouth open, tears running down her face, staring at Felix. She has done the maths, as they say. 'Bastard,' she says, and turns away. I hear rather than see her go through the door.

Felix pulls Amanda's arm, forcing her to turn around, presses her back against the railing and says again, 'Tell him.'

'Dan is right,' she says, 'You mean nothing to me. It was a fling, one of many.'

'He's got to you,' he hisses into her face. 'But I won't give up, ever. You and me, it's forever.'

The disembodied astrologer says, 'Ladies and gentlemen, we have totality.'

Two minutes and forty-seven seconds to put my world back on its axis. We work together, Amanda and me. Choreographed by a life as lovers and parents, we sense what we cannot see in one another's movements in the twilight. Amanda slips under Felix's arm and I push him against the railing.

Last night, we talked about the boys when they were little. We remembered Drew, learning to do the forward roll. We taught him how to place his hands either side, tuck his head in, bend over, lift his bottom, get to tipping point, let the body go, and roll. Once he got the hang of it, he wouldn't stop. He rolled everywhere—up and down the garden, from one room to another, into bed— he became quite the gymnast.

Our eyes meet over Felix's head as I push it down, so he is looking at the waves. Instinctively, he grips the railing either side of him. Amanda takes his nearest hand in hers. I feel him relax slightly, thinking she's helping him, and his other hand loosens its hold, so I can push his head further forward. It's a simple thing, then, to lift his legs with my free arm. For all his height, he's not heavy. A lightweight. That shouldn't surprise me. He reaches tipping point; I feel his legs slip through my hands, and he becomes a shadow receding, dropping into the dark waves. We put on our eclipse viewers and join in the cries of wonderment, looking up to see the corona encircle the moon.

Driving Blind
Jennifer Bailey

After her sister's death from a heart attack, my mother moved in with my uncle. The fall-out was a tangle of questions my father took to repeating; for example, how long had they been carrying on, had my aunt been driven to her unexpected death, and had all this caused their adopted daughter's emigration to Cape Town? My father came up with new questions daily, which I was learning to ignore, though not because I was unaffected by the change in our lives. But I try to be forward-looking. And although it's necessary to begin with these few facts, since I've nothing to hide, they're only a backdrop to what happened next.

When we left the north, my father and me, the city had long been in my sights. Plus I was trying to take care of his life though neither of us was old enough for this kind of routine, me only five years out of college and my father on early retirement from the force due to the state of his lungs.

On an evening after work I was driving east through suburbia and ignoring Florence's voice which was programmed to the coordinates of home. Her steady reprimands gave me an illusion of control because the truth was, I'd no destination. This was practice driving. My biggest fear was getting lost in the city, and I aimed to overcome it.

There had been a period of hot humid weather and now the sky deepened to navy, lightening flickered, thunder cracked overhead and the rain came on fast and heavy. I winced when the wipers scraped across the windscreen.

I'd reached a high street of greased lights and people skittering with and without umbrellas, hemmed in behind crash barriers. A dog crazed through traffic. The bus ahead mounted the kerb as it veered left. A roundabout took me onto a dual carriageway. Traffic surged, there was a confusion of lane-changing, a fly-over, and the sky hurled rain. My knees quivered, and I made for the first exit into a tangle of streets and one-way arrows. Gutters overflowed from stopped-up drains as if the road was about to flood and engulf the car till it was lifted, tilted, submerged.

Breaking news announced a bomb explosion in the city's financial district. I switched off the wipers, imagined upended concrete slabs smoking in the wet, zipped and hooded my waterproof to take a recce of the locality for street names to locate later on the map. Then Florence took me home.

I'd found us a ground floor rented flat, shabby and hard work to keep clean, though the rooms were large, big-windowed and from the front, looked out onto a tree-lined Square. That night, the doorbell woke me and for a while I lay, not daring to move. The rain had stopped. A car passed, tyres hissing, and I slept again, this time more deeply than I thought possible.

Like he did every morning, my father woke me with tea, always too weak, the sugar piled in though I drank it. He dragged back the curtains which showed a low heavy sky. The windows sounded a steady vibration from invisible planes on their landing trajectories. It was Saturday so my father sat on the bed. We exchanged memories of the evening and night, till the coughing took him again and he left for the bathroom.

'I should've never given you the money for that car.'

'Six thousand. Show me something as reliable for less. And you didn't.'

'What are you talking about?'

'Alright. The down payment.'

'Gratitude would be nice.'

'You've already had that.'

'What do I do if you don't come back?'

'I left you a voice mail.'

'You know I can't hear those things.'

'It's always about you. What's your scenario for me?'

'Dead. Buried under some bloody truck.'

I offered him a mutilated face tilted over a broken neck and he shook his head.

'Pitiful.'

He said he hadn't heard the doorbell.

'Joanie, I think you dreamed the sound.'

I replayed its harsh echo.

We always ate eggs for breakfast, my father's hard boiled and mashed in butter and pepper, mine poached. The bomb was headline news. No-one had been killed and though a whole floor was blown out, the building had held. I thought how reason had gone to the dogs so it was all about gods of whatever stripe that put paid to conscience. Conscience though, could have you in a strait-jacket.

My father shelled his egg, weighed the soft ovoid in his palm then tipped it into a bowl with butter, which melted slowly. He stared at his hands while one held the bowl and the other pressed a fork to begin the mash. I went out, emptied teapot dregs in the garden and watched the wind lash horse chestnuts in the Square, their leaves and candles ripping air. The cloud thinned and in places broke to show sharp spears of sunlight and the drifting planes.

To smooth over our morning stand-off, I took my father for an easy walk. From the supermarket car park, we followed a path across small thistling fields, hedges of blossoming hawthorn and blackberry, tree thickets, all sheltered by motorway flyovers which I hadn't yet learned how to access. Traffic hummed. Long grasses flicked my knees. We rested often so my father could cough, spit, clear his lungs and wait for his pulse to slow. The sky had turned super bright and gave off a shimmering effect. I checked my phone and there were two texts which I couldn't read in the light.

We smelled then saw smoke and followed it to a clearing where a fire burned inside a circle of stones. My father sat on one and leaned forward for breath. I knelt next to him, taking the heat on my face, breathing in smoke, feeling the pain of it in my eyes which wept. My father stirred.

'We'll need to be off before they're back.'

'Who've you got in mind?'

He stretched his fingers but otherwise didn't move.

'It's alright here. I've sometimes wondered...'

A man walked from the tree thicket. My father stood and stepped back. I crouched, ready to move. When the man reached us, he nodded, placed a sketch pad on one of the stones and there was my father resting and me kneeling by the fire, the pencil lines quick and hazed and true.

My father's lips pursed.

'By god, that's good.'

The man nodded. I hated what he'd done. Pointed at the sketch.

'That's an exercise in spying.'

My father shouted me down but in wide deliberate movements, the man tore the drawing four ways and threw it in his fire. That's what he said, sounding breathless, that the fire was his.

I recognised him. In the Square of three storey Victorian houses, his was a few doors down, the only one I knew of that hadn't been converted to flats. The front garden had a high fir tree tapering down to splayed branches which concealed the windows. The garden itself was neglected but not overgrown, though I'd never seen anyone working there. He came and went through an ornate iron gate and I suppose I learned to remember him for the way he walked, like a heavy animal balancing on hind legs, and how that made him look vulnerable. Close up, I saw he was younger than I thought, his face made striking by a large narrow nose and heavy lips. I found a stick and scattered the paper ashes, impressed by his destruction. He'd turned his back on us.

I took my father's arm. Once on his feet, he pushed me off.

'You're a nuisance, Joanie.'

We were near home when he spoke again.

'That fire's a hazard. I don't even think it's legal.'

The man's name was Michael. He joined me while I was working outside on the car, so I turned to face him.

'Joan.'

He said something. Though I was conditioned by now to the planes, a lawn mower's whine had joined the squawks of manic parakeets.

'What?'

'There's a mechanic round the corner.'

'I'm on a level 2 Diploma in Car Mechanics.'

'Why did you...'

'Currently repair competence and principles so I'm practising how to remove and replace engine parts.'

'So why?'

'There's no mystery to machines, they work according to set principles. And if they don't you repair them or chuck them for scrap. Simple.'

None of which had occurred to me until I'd moved to the city.

Michael looked unconvinced. He didn't seem slow but I couldn't sense an edge to this man. He leaned from the hips as if about to topple. His T shirt was shapeless and like his jeans, grubbed with paint.

'Give me time and I'll be that guy round the corner.'

'OK.' He shrugged. 'I don't drive.'

The lawn mower stopped, the parakeets had moved on. I thought I should try and equal things between us.

'Your house is quite something. All that space. Is there just you to fill it?' This last was pushy but I thought the admiring tone would swing it.

'It belonged to my grandparents and then parents.' Like before, his breathing was full of effort. 'I've always lived here.'

'That's pretty weird.'

He looked straight at me, showed his teeth which were big and strong looking.

'Not everyone has to see things your way.'

He was right. Maybe I should've said so but instead focussed on the ignition system, cancelling the chance of another street-level conversation.

Wrong. It set a routine where Michael managed an opening remark and I joined in long enough to stoke his anger, which never stopped him from coming back. I didn't mind. It was like shuffle-dancing with a bear.

The days were lengthening fast so when I next took to driving blind, there was still a hectic blush over the skyline. I came across and followed motorway signs, made the leap and headed south, Florence announcing pointless directions.

It was easier than I'd thought. Driving the slow lane, I switched off Florence, relaxed into a surge of happy thoughts. Such as how it had been a step in the right direction to move down here, give my father the opportunity to find his feet. Such as how clever I'd been to buy the Micra; red paintwork I kept to a shine, eight years old, thirty one and a half thousand on the clock and running smoothly . Also, trying not to hold a grudge, I'd sent my mother a friendly email.

I kept to a steady sixty. The day had gone, a fat moon climbing the sky clear of cloud, nothing to see either side but empty landscapes, then a siren approaching, and I was losing the happy thoughts. Blue lights pulsed in the rear view mirror, wing mirror, near-side window on the hard shoulder, police and ambulance. Traffic slowed and stopped.

I switched on Florence. It was five miles to an exit which would get me home, so I checked the location, recorded that and the date in my notebook then phoned my father who of course didn't answer though I left a message anyway. People, mostly men, wandered the traffic. A fat guy in T shirt and shorts walked with purpose down the line of cars, and talked to drivers who'd rolled down their windows, like he was in the know and not some bored no-body. When he got close, I pulled out my training manual and got busy-looking.

Two hours and twenty two minutes later I was funnelled into the outside lane, cranking forward, first gear, handbrake, first gear. And here was the disaster, announced by arc lights that revealed, detail by detail for each yard covered, an upended car with its door open to the sky, another two in a mess of metal, an intact motorcycle tipped to its side as if parked. An ambulance, blood on the tarmac. But not mine; not mine.

The following evening Michael was perched on a low wall that fronted the flat; comfortable looking, he sketched the horse chestnuts. He said my father had banged on his door when I hadn't returned from the drive, not that my father mentioned it while shouting me down.

I apologised for him, said he was a fool not picking up the phone or checking voicemail. Angry on cue,

Michael defended him blah blah. I was moving past, tired to the bone, when he broke routine and invited me to his house. For what he didn't say. Food, booze, a tour or sex which I was ready to consider because I'd already decided Michael could be one of those people who looked better without clothes. But nervy because I didn't and it'd been quite a while.

We fixed the invite for Saturday. The wind blew cold enough for a sweater over my overalls while I spent the afternoon with car innards, mainly the oil system, lined along the kerb. Michael came out, not to watch or talk but draw. I allowed that now because he asked and besides, like my father said, he was good; enough to make me laugh at the quickness of his hand across paper and how the drawing carried movement as well as something in my face I hadn't seen before but liked anyway.

That day he gave me one which I showed my father who said he would get a frame for it.

'You look better on paper. The lad's flattered you.'

He glanced between me in work clothes and the drawing as if I was living under a false identity.

'You know nothing,' I said.

'Isn't it worth taking a bit of trouble for the evening? I've kept a nice dress that belonged to your mother.'

'Wear it yourself.'

Michael lived as if electricity had been invented for lights only; no TV, computer, or any kind of music system or phone I could see. Just lamps, a crystal chandelier, sconces, an LED angle-poise clamped to a big wooden desk painted blue and covered with books, fabric swatches, mugs holding stale tea, brushes, pencils, flowers, a tarnished Buddha, some more flowers that were dead, the torso of a plastic doll, a man's shoe. Stuff. And that was just the desk. Everywhere in his sitting room, on furniture, shelves and floor, more stuff including a dress maker's mannequin. As well as stacked canvases and an easel, what you'd expect.

The real shock was four large paintings of me hung in a row over the fireplace. In one of them the woman wore a sleeveless dress patterned with flowers. She faced a mirror reflecting an exact image. Her raised right arm exposed a smudge of dark hair.

He waited. I stared. There was a surface resemblance but these women were lofty in their downward look.

'Well?'

'I shave my armpits.'

'Anything else?'

But Michael had cornered me to a silence I couldn't break. He said there would be an exhibition in the local library and I told him he could show anything but the one with the flowered dress. I expected him to question that but he nodded and thanked me.

A statue of the Virgin bigger than life size stood in an alcove along a corridor to the kitchen. Her blue veil was chipped, a finger missing, a stack of books at her feet. Michael said his grandmother had been a convert but no-one else followed suit. I sidled past, wading through the Virgin's shadow, and watched him taste something from a pan.

He said, 'You must dislike this chaos.'

'Says who?'

'Well everything you take out of your car is arranged in a pattern on the ground. The car itself is glossy, the interior looks untouched as if you're about to move in.'

'When my father gets huffy I've thought of it.'

Not saying it wasn't huffiness; rather the hours of coughing, hoiking phlegm, spitting, which could take place in the kitchen sink as much as the bathroom sink or toilet. Me forever having to clean after him. And I couldn't persuade him to take a bath instead of standing in the kitchen stripped to the waist and thinking that was enough.

'I'm not criticising.'

'What a relief. Otherwise I'd not have been able to sleep for the worry.'

Michael breathed fast, his eyebrows on a worried slope.

'Joke,' I said.

'I've been keeping your father company.'

'His idea or yours?'

'He's lonely.'

I felt ready to dump my father on a central reservation but said nothing.

Michael's hands shook opening a bottle of wine. We drank that with his stew and potatoes at the Formica kitchen table, candles lit, dirty pans piled and shadowed against the ceiling. Now and again he left off eating and reached for my hand while I waited till he gave it back.

There was no shortage of conversation. Michael had these questions and the minute I finished answering one, he came in with the next as if from a list he'd compiled earlier. I gave him a woman who managed the office of a car dealership, who'd learned to drive on a tractor, needing a stack of cushions to reach the steering wheel. I threw in a step-father with a habit of exposing himself, this last out of curiosity. Michael took this as a cue to reach for my hand again.

When we finished eating, left the kitchen mess for the stuff of his sitting room and a roomy sofa that faced away from Michael's paintings, the wine helped me off with my blouse. I reached back to unhook my bra, but he stopped my arm. So I kissed him, leaning at an awkward angle to cover the space between us, and began to unbutton his shirt. He held me off. I thought it could be the lights and got up to switch everything off but a single corner lamp on the floor. He waited till I'd finished then stood and gave me the blouse. It was inside out and I tore a side seam pulling it to the right side. He gripped my shoulders so I had to stop moving.

'It's alright, Joan. Joanie.'

His breathing sounded painful. I tried to get loose but he had a tight grip.

'Why d'you light fires?'

'I like to get out in the open, though your father's right, a fire's too risky.'

He pressed me against his chest, his face in my hair, saying things I wasn't meant to hear. The moment he relaxed, I pulled clear.

'There's a meringue for pudding.'

'Sorry. Time I was off.'

He watched me leave, his arm raised, his fingers plucking air.

There was another hot spell, far enough into summer for grass to yellow, earth to turn dusty, trees to drop conkers. The sky was pale blue fading to early evening grey when I silenced Florence and drove west, following the planes, dreaming the moment of their dropped landing gear, steering between lanes on the city exit roads, going fast. Turning for the airport, overhead engines had me ducking. I followed the perimeter road, slowing to third gear, hugging the wheel, driving alongside steel-white cargo buildings, an Esso station, wire-topped boundary hoarding. The sun smudged my line of sight, then I swerved to join a line of cars parked where the verge rose to a grassed embankment.

The watchers held binoculars, cameras, iPhones, take-out lattes, not silent but not saying much either. And here it all was. A jewelled light, yellow in a darkening sky, a balanced descent, a vast scuff onto land, the sequence repeated and repeated. Each time I would think it the last but then there was the next one and the next one. I might've made a crying sound because the girl next to me offered a cigarette then a session on her flight radar app. I said no to both and she smiled. It was OK. Her boyfriend took photos and wrote in a marbled hard-back notebook.

After a while I lay back on the flattened grass and lulled by engine blasts and wafts of diesel, closed my eyes. I must've slept. It was dark, the embankment had emptied and the planes encrusted with landing lights waxed into view. I watched them, over and over, letting the rhythm settle me, not thinking of their turn at the runway's end when they crawled to a stand and emptied.

I'd been ready to wait for dawn when a policeman led me back to the Micra. He checked my license and registration, searched the car and followed me off the perimeter road. It was while he searched, pushing his fingers between seat cushions, that my phone rang. I didn't recognise the number and though the policeman told me not to answer, I knew who was there, waiting to hear me speak, but when I checked there was no message.

I reached home at twelve thirty five. The front room window was lit, curtains undrawn. I sat on the garden wall and watched my father and Michael talking, their armchairs facing and pulled close to each other. My father shifted to rearrange his trousers. Michael held a biscuit. I felt hunger when he bit into the biscuit, catching crumbs in his other hand. My father coughed. I thought I could hear their voices and the far-off whistle of a kettle for tea. Wanting to leave, I couldn't move.

Pink Knickers
Mandy Huggins

I saw you today. I passed by the barber shop in town, and there you were in a chair by the window. You looked exactly as I remembered, but ten years older, your broad nose still freckled, and that same easy grin as you chatted to the girl cutting your hair. Shamelessly flirting; talking with your hands and your eyes. I paused at the window for a moment, hoping you'd look up.

Then reality kicked in; there was no way that it could have been you. And even if there had been that possibility, it's over forty years since I last saw you. You'd be fifty-four now, not twenty-four.

In 1974 I was thirteen and you were fourteen. I wasn't allowed to hang out with you. You were on my mother's 'that' list, right up there in the top ten thats. 'That Ian Armstrong,' tempting and forbidden.

I wasn't allowed to go into the disused quarry either, but one afternoon in the summer holidays I found myself stuck halfway up the cliff face, my plimsolls mired in heavy clay. The yellow-grey mud was underneath my fingernails and in my hair; smeared across my jeans and jacket.

And I was frightened. You were shouting from above; encouraging and threatening in equal measure.

I couldn't let you see I was scared. But there was no way up and no way down. I clung hopelessly to a thin branch of broom and felt the tears well up as the thorns bit into my palms.

Then you were stretching down; reaching out for me with your sticky grey hand. I held it tightly and hauled myself up those last few feet to the top. With a last pull, you saw me safely over the overhang, and then abruptly let go and flung yourself down onto the thick couch grass.

I had never been up there before. I could see into the back gardens of the council houses that ran along the edge of the field beyond the quarry, and up on the top were a row of sheds and neatly marked out allotments.

You jumped up.

'Come on,' you said, 'let's go and see what we can find.'

You walked over to the first shed and peered through the window with your hand cupped against the glass. There was no one around, but the allotments were all well-tended. This one had rows of peas, pale green lettuces and thick-skinned broad beans. Honeysuckle climbed a trellis on the fence.

You tried the door to the shed, which was held by a small padlock. You pulled it half-heartedly, and shrugged.

'Nothing much in there anyway,' you said.

I admit I was relieved. I didn't want you to take anything.

At the end of the row of allotments there was a stack of stuff piled into a makeshift bonfire, next to a large compost heap. On the bonfire there was an old washstand. Its marble top had been hacked off and left at the side, but there were still patterned tiles on the wooden splash-back. They were decorated with flowers; deep red tulips with fleshy leaves. I ran my fingers over the raised pattern.

You looked over my shoulder.

'Do you want one?' you asked.

I nodded.

'What's it worth?'

I could feel my heart thudding. This whey my mother told me not to speak to you or any of your friends. She always said you would want me to do things I didn't want to do; things that I mustn't let you do.

84

But I wanted the tile.

'I'll let you kiss me,' I said, feeling my cheeks flush. I looked at your mouth as I said it, wondering how it would taste on mine. I imagined your hot mid-afternoon breath tasting of dunked biscuits, malty and sweet.

I was a late starter. I'd only kissed a boy once; Kevin Wastling behind the dusty velvet curtains at the school dance. Do you remember him? He had a pasty complexion and home-knitted gloves fastened to his duffle-coat pockets with plaited wool.

But in the giddy excitement of my first dance, he seemed attractive in his new blue shirt and Levis. His hand was warm in mine as he led me over to the long curtains by the window. And behind those curtains, with my back pressed awkwardly against the sharp metal window frame, we kissed all night. They were kisses for kissing's sake. They weren't meant to arouse passion or express love. They were exploratory kisses. Kisses that were meant for tasting, for rolling around the mouth and savouring. They were kisses that simply led to more kisses. Kisses that made my mouth sore, kisses that made my tongue swell. Beautiful teenage kisses.

But when I said you could kiss me, you looked at me oddly.

You got out your small penknife and slid the blade down between the top tile and the cracked wood backing. I saw it give slightly, and you flexed the knife. Then you stopped and looked at me again, squinting against the sun.

'Let me put my hand in your knickers,' you said.

It was a statement, not a question. That was the price of the tile. I didn't feel I had a choice, and I didn't want one. It was exciting to be up there with you, watching the sunlight dance on your soft brown hair.

'OK,' I whispered.

You took my hand and led me round the back of the shed where the honeysuckle was growing. There was a single sunflower in a pot, its head hanging heavy with the fullness and weight of its seeds.

'Lie down over there,' you said.

I shook my head.

'Tile first.'

'Wait here then.'

I could have run, I could have changed my mind, and I know you would have just shrugged and smiled. But I waited for you to come back, inhaling the heady scent of the honeysuckle, telling myself that it would be alright.

You returned with two tiles. They were beautiful. Deep, deep green, purple and crimson. Crackled, crazed glaze. You threw them down on the grass next to me.

'Lie down then,' you said.

I lay down without a word.

You flopped down next to me and wiped the clay off your hands as best you could, without me having to ask. Then you leant over and kissed me. It was a clumsy kiss, your teeth grating against mine, your tongue trying to find a way inside my mouth. You tasted of summer and earth.

When I felt your hand on my stomach I jumped. You left it there a moment until I lay still, and I decided to let you do whatever you wanted.

You unfastened my jeans and pushed your hand inside my knickers. I felt your fingers dance lightly across my skin, almost tickling, and I held my breath until you took your hand out. You muttered something that sounded like 'thanks'.

I was disappointed. I thought I would feel different in some way, yet I was still Sandra, laid in the grass with my pink cotton knickers on show.

But I had something good to tell Maria and Susan. I had gone further with a boy than they had, and I knew Susan would be jealous.

And I had the tiles, the beautiful tiles with the art deco flowers. But I didn't know where I would tell my mother I had got them from, or how I'd explain the clay on my new pink knickers.

I wanted to keep you up there a while longer, so I reached into my jacket pocket for the Rizla tin with the rolling machine in the lid. The one that I had stolen from my dad's drawer the last time I was there. Maria had brought round some of her granddad's tobacco, and we had been practicing rolling cigarettes in my bedroom.

I passed the tin to you, but you pushed it back across the grass to me.

'Roll one for me will you?' you said.

You lay back down, crossing your arms behind your head and closing your eyes against the sun. Even though you weren't watching, my hand shook as I took a liquorice paper from the packet and a finger of tobacco from the tin.

You held the finished cigarette up and examined it with a grin.

'Not bad.'

You smoked it as though it was a special cigar, holding it out and examining it between drags. I loved you for that. That was the moment I knew.

Then you reached for my hand to pull me up, and I felt a shiver run through me.

'Can we come up here again?' I asked.

You smiled. That bemused, lop-sided smile.

'Yes, Sandra Broadbent,' you said, 'we can come up here again.'

You started to clamber down the cliff ahead of me, and I stumbled after you, trying to hide my daft grin. But you rushed ahead, slipping and sliding down the clay bank without looking back.

I started to slide down behind you, clutching the tiles and reaching out for a tuft of couch grass with my free hand.I wanted to call out and ask you to help me, but it came out as a squeak, and you were disappearing below the ridge.

I couldn't stop myself from falling any longer, and as the thick slick of clay fell away beneath me, I screamed.You turned to look at me just as I dropped one of the tiles. It went flying over the edge of the ridge, and as you ducked, I saw your head hit a tree stump, and you lay still.

I slid past you and came to a stop in the blackberry bushes at the bottom. I lay there for a minute. My left leg hurt and the thorns were jabbing into my arm. The remaining tile lay at the side of me, cracked, but still in one piece.

I was scared, but I knew that I couldn't stay there, that no one would find us if I didn't get help. I stood, and tested my leg. I had twisted it, but I instinctively knew that it wasn't broken. I also knew that you were badly hurt, and that consequently I was in serious trouble. But you weren't a grass, and I figured that if I dialled 999 anonymously I could save my own bacon.

In the telephone box at the end of the road I turned the dial round to 9. Then I paused as I caught sight of my reflection in the glass. My arms and legs were smeared with thick yellow clay. I'd messed with the big boys and I was about to be caught out. I would be in the worst trouble of my life. I let go of the dial abruptly, and reached up to replace the receiver.

But as I was about to put it down I snatched it back. I couldn't leave you there. I turned the dial round twice more to nine, and whispered directions to the operator as to where to send an ambulance. I wouldn't tell them my name. Then I ran home, getting there just minutes before my mother was due back from work. I hid my clothes under the bed, took fresh jeans from the drawer and quickly ran a bath. As I climbed into the water I heard the ambulance tear by on its way to the hospital.

It was only much later that evening that I remembered the tile. I had left it in the phone box, on the shelf with the directories.

I went back the next day, but it had gone. So I walked around the bottom of the cliffs to see if I could find the other tile; the one that had slipped from my hand. It was there, miraculously unbroken. I carried it home and hid it under the bed with my dirty clothes.

When the local paper asked for the girl who had called the ambulance to come forward, my mother didn't say a word. But I knew she knew.

Two weeks later I took the tile to the cemetery, wrapped in my pink knickers, and laid it with the wilting flowers on the raw mound of your grave.

This is for You

L F Roth

'Listen to this,' he says. He runs his hand along the strings inside the old upright, making it sound like a harp but with more of a twang. 'You hear?'

He never took lessons.

'Were you polishing it?' she asks. He has folded back the top. It is divided in two, lengthwise; four hinges hold the sections together. This is the first time she has seen him near it.

'No. I was wondering what it looked like inside.'

'There are strings and hammers,' she tells him.

'I know that. I wanted a peep.'

Sometimes he is so childlike.

It is his piano. Joan never wanted it. When his uncle died, no one had any use for it so Gerald took it. 'I'll learn to play next year when I retire,' he had said, always the optimist. She had objected, pointing out how big it was: it would dwarf everything in the room. If he wanted an instrument, he could get one of those small digital keyboards that were so popular. But he had made up his mind and she yielded. At least it was better than the choice of some retirees she has heard of, a Harley-Davidson, if barely—with its cast iron frame it no doubt weighs about the same. It is stationary, though. He won't kill himself rounding some curve. At the funeral, where the shiny black coffin, surrounded by wreaths and flowers, reminded her of the piano, she'd thought she might be able to hide it behind a wall of aspidistras, creating an indoor bower of sorts that she need never visit.

Actually, what troubled her was less its size than the memories that surfaced with it, tainting its arrival, but this she did not tell him. Unlike Gerald, she had taken lessons as a child. No older than eleven or twelve, she had had no say in the matter. Had she but known, a clichéd phrase she learned appeared with some frequency in the whodunnits that her parents read; had she but known what would follow, what crime, for so she viewed it, would be perpetrated on her, she might have—indeed, she would have—put up a fight. Not that it would have helped. She was at that in-between stage of no resistance, neither small enough to be able to resort to temper tantrums at home and abroad, shaming her parents into backing down, nor yet a teenager combining the will of a two-year-old with the strength of an adult. But she did not know.

Oh, the bitterness that the instrument evokes.

She leaves Gerald playing at playing and goes out into the garden. There is weeding to be done, a more congenial five-finger exercise that might take her mind off the drills she suffered through as a child. Gloved, she picks up a trowel and gets a cushion; she works diligently, kneeling as she starts out but soon half-seated, to save her knees. Whatever she does not recognise, whatever comes without a name, she treats as a weed. Before long there is a small pile beside her.

It does not help, though.

If she could put her memories in a pile and bury them, that might.

Miss Griffith—that was her name. Funny how some names stick. Or was it Griffiths? No, Griffith. A mouthful either way. Not that Joan had had to use the name; yes, miss, no, miss, was all that was required.

Yes, miss. No, miss. Yes, miss, I'll try.

The last, modified version she learned to avoid. Whether or not Miss Griffith was familiar with Matthew 5, any attempt to qualify a yes or no was quickly stifled: '… let your communication be, Yea, yea; Nay, nay …'

Vulturelike—is this really true?—her cold eyes signalled disapproval; there was no need for words to reinforce the message.

Joan shivers, less at some actual memory than at the picture she has conjured up. She takes off her gloves to move a strand of hair out of her face before going back to weeding.

But the image of her teacher returns.

The early sessions left little trace. What she had to learn was relatively simple: brief exercises and a few tunes long since familiar. Reading music was new, naturally, but appeared uncomplicated: a mere fraction of the keyboard was used—her hands, and mostly only one initially, were kept within the confines of one octave; there were no sharps or flats; each note was one, two or four beats, nothing more complex; and though their names must have been used, crotchet, minim, whatever, she had paid scant attention so they never troubled her.

But over time, as the lessons progressed, she herself failed to do so. What she remembers from the years that followed is her own ineptitude—and Miss Griffith's impatience.

'Stop,' she would say. 'Stop right there. Your whole body is tense. You must learn to relax.' She would grab Joan's hand. 'Your wrists have to be supple.' And to achieve the desired suppleness she would bash the offending hand against the keys, keeping time with her command: 'Relax. Relax. Relax.'

But how could Joan relax? When the music in front of her had the appearance of a minefield, each note a mine, its position at times confused by sharps and flats to be found not where the note stood but to the far left, by the clef; when each note or chord had its own value, forcing her to keep count; when some had additional symbols attached to them, adding or cancelling information; when often whole sets of notes had escaped the lines that held the rest and were to be found high above or far below them, on a separate line or set of lines, to indicate—and force her to calculate—its place in the system, as if she had nothing else to do—how could she relax?

Even at home, where she had time to figure out, pencil in hand, which key to press down, she was likely to go wrong. What sounded fine to her was very often not what the composer had intended. 'D?' Miss Griffith would say, her intonation stressing the absurdity of what she had heard. 'D? Where do you find that?' And not too sure exactly where she had played a D, Joan's hand would hover while she searched the field until Miss Griffith grabbed it and made it land on the keyboard in the vicinity of the A she should have played, resulting in both pain and dissonance.

Joan stabs at a root. Too late she sees it is an aster, not a weed. She shrugs. The asters can do with thinning anyway. She starts a second pile beside the weeds. Once she is done, she'll pick a few to bring indoors.

Mistakes, she knows, will happen if you are in a rush, in music as in gardening. Strange that she never simply took it in her stride. At school, she was fed the teacherly platitude used to pat slow learners on the back: you can't improve unless you make mistakes. Miss Griffith proffered no consolation. Would it have helped Joan if she had, or, alternatively, if her mistakes had been ignored? Joan doubts it. When her fingers got entangled; when she very obviously hit the wrong note; when she was completely stuck, she knew, and knowing never shrugged it off as a necessary step in order to learn. Pieces marked *adagio* and *lento* she could negotiate, if barely. But with tempos like *allegro* and *vivace*, even though Miss Griffith spared her the metronome, she grew hot and uncomfortable, playing as if she was wearing mittens on both hands. And *allegrissimo*, if she had ever had the misfortune to encounter it, would have made her bury her musical trowel full force in the nearest hornets' nest.

What Miss Griffith did not spare her was playing four-handed, a cruel exercise, always involving music she had neither seen nor heard before. 'Would you move over to the left, please,' Miss Griffith would say and Joan knew immediately what she was in for. Why did the left page, with the lower pitch, generally the bass, always fall on her? There were fewer notes to play and fewer complicated sequences, it is true, but as a consequence there were also a great many places where she had to pause for one or more beats, long rests indicated by dashes suspended from or reposing on the line, as if that could make much difference, short ones by squiggles that caused problems of their own. When was she to play the next note? She never knew. She never knew till the moment Miss Griffith slowed down markedly to spur her on and then, not hiding her exasperation, drew to a halt. And as if those problems were not enough, more notes than ever were submerged in the depths, far below the few she had finally learned to master, secured as they were on or between the lines—though to claim mastery was perhaps wishful thinking. As often as not she still missed sharps and flats.

'What key are we playing in?' Miss Griffith would ask and Joan would know that that was not the question.

'D?' she would suggest, a common key.

'So where do you find that?'

Joan's eyes would roam in search of a letter that might be the key to the key.

The prompt would be terse.

'Look at the last note.'

Often there wasn't one. 'There are three,' she would say, looking at the chord, her confusion growing.

'You go by the bass note.'

'A,' she would say.

G it would be.

'And how many sharps are there in G major?'

Two? Three? Joan would guess wildly, even though she knew. She really did.

All that to tell her she had played an F instead of an F#.

And so it went.

Joan looks at the flower in her left hand, where there should have been a weed. The humiliation she felt is with her even today, after so many years. She was ignorant, no two ways about it, and made to feel more so—made to remain the weed she was. Unable to focus clearly, she looks at the pile she has been adding to and finds more asters there: three ... four ... five. She shouldn't get so involved in the past. Gently she separates them from the weeds and places them beside the flower she cut down first. Perhaps she will be able to transplant a few from places where they grow too close and fill the gaps.

Predictably, with hindsight, her reaction had been to resort to subterfuge. She feels bad about this too: wiliness is not a trait she admires—well, who does?—but has her defence prepared. She was trying to protect herself. Nor did she turn into a hardened criminal, playing truant, defiantly. Twice, twice, that was all, she made use of a stratagem, telling her parents she had hurt her wrist—the wrist not supple enough for Miss Griffith —by falling, being pushed, in the gym. No need for details. No need for a doctor either; most likely it was no more than a sprain. She would be fine in a few weeks. And she was—until the next time, less than a year later. What unwilling piano pupil has not done the same?

Joan pulls at a root that is protruding from the edge of the flowerbed in order to remove it. It won't yield, so she hacks at it, repeating Miss Griffith's exercise to get her to loosen up. Weeding might have made her a better pianist. She smiles but dismisses the thought. Practice might have. A reluctant pupil, she often put off practising as long as possible, if not in fact entirely. As a result, once or twice, never routinely, she had presented the previous week's assignment as her new homework—Miss Griffith had so many pupils that she was unlikely to keep track of them all. Had she even erased the date on one or two occasions, the date Miss Griffith generally pencilled beside the title of a new piece? She is not sure. She pats down the soil where the root had been.

Enough for today. Joan lets go of the trowel, gathers the weeds in her arms and takes them to the compost bin. When she returns, she removes her gloves. She picks up the seven asters that fell victim to her inattentiveness. Tomorrow she will try and move some that are still in bud to fill their places. It might work.

Inside, there is no Gerald—he must have gone out the front. She leaves the flowers beside the sink and heads for the living room. There the top of the piano is still open. She walks over to close it but changes her mind. Instead she pulls out the stool, sits down and lifts the lid that covers the keys. There are eighty-eight of them, she knows, where twenty-four, two octaves, would have kept her busy—perhaps even content.

Could things have worked out differently? No prodigy, could she have learned to play? There is no knowing. It is easy to blame Miss Griffith. She was the teacher, and the adult. But where were Joan's parents? Why didn't they see what was going on and put a stop to it? More to the point, why didn't she herself speak up? Or did she? She must have complained, surely, or was she too well brought up, too well-behaved? Is that the reason she lied, and went on lying, about her homework? Well-behaved and devious both.

Frustrated she hits the keys with her two hands simultaneously, her wrists not the least relaxed, producing a clamour, a cacophony of sound. She pushes down on the sustain pedal with her right foot and keeps it down, hitting the keys a second time, a third. 'This is for you,' she says, and then repeats the phrase again and again, louder and louder, ending up shouting at the top of her voice while pounding the keys, no longer knowing who she is addressing: 'This is for you! This is for you!' Only when she is out of breath does she stop. She slumps over the keyboard. The echo lingers.

When she looks up, Gerald is standing in the doorway.

'I'll get rid of it,' he says, quietly. 'I didn't know how you felt.'

'It's all right,' she tells him. 'It won't happen again. I'm done.'

And she gets up. The flowers in the kitchen will need water. She has to find them a vase. At least she can do that much.

Restoration
by Aoife Fitzpatrick

I can see them from the corner of my eye—Terence and
Stella nudging their two girls. They're trying to stop them
from staring at my phenomenal hands. As I pour the tea,
the children are amazed to see that my extremities do
not, in fact, belong at the top of a beanstalk. They are my
greatest gifts, supple and elegant and capable of great
refinement in the dispensing of beverages.

'Battenberg?' I say, the china ringing as I set the teapot
down to proffer a stack of pink and yellow squares.

Stella shoots a coded glance at Terence and he rubs
his knees in sham indecision.

'Ah, no, thanks,' he says. 'We're not staying long.'

I am Hades offering pomegranate seeds. They believe
cake to be a stratagem of the elderly, a lure to swindle
company out of the young. I stand with the plate in my
vast palm while they look embarrassed for me, caught
red-handed trying to trap them in my underworld.

This has been our routine since Annie died. Twice a
year, Terence darkens my door—once in the summer
with Pimms and again at Christmas with what I will
admit is a decent Armagnac. We talk about his mother
mostly, though he seems to have little interest in that part
of her life before he was born, as if she were not quite
legitimate or manifest until he was conceived.

I ease myself onto the armchair and air issues coarsely
from the leather cushion. The girls snicker, little
shoulders twitching. Terence finds this charming and
beams at me. I try to look enchanted, but effect the
bemusement of the hard of hearing.

'So,' I say. 'Do you have Annie's scarf?' I feel my vigorous eyebrows rise and hope that my tone isn't too desperate. 'You know ... the paisley one?'

Stella stares into space. The question seems to roll around her head like a marble until it finally drops into a slot. 'Oh, that,' she says, fingertips tracing the worn-gold rim of her cup. 'No.'

'Not sure where it is.' Terence rocks forwards to claim his tea, and in the moment that it takes to resettle his backside, the subject is closed.

It is like the stun of a slap, though no hand has been laid upon me. Terence's face is set with maddening certainty, an expression contrived to deny what I know— that the scarf is tied to the rail in his wardrobe. He told me so only at Christmas. He loves the bitter draft of oakmoss released from the silk every time it's disturbed, and he thought that this decaying note was a vestige of the perfume that his father gave to Annie on their wedding day. But the truth, as I explained it, is that both the scarf and the scent were gifts from me—not to mark my little sister's marriage, but to celebrate her twenty-first birthday.

This coming of age fell on the same day as my first solo recital—a lunchtime affair at the Royal Academy, made all the more nerve-wracking because Annie arrived from Dublin to watch me. She sat neatly cross-legged in the front row while my unparalleled span eased over the keys, through Fauré's layers of arpeggios and sparkling runs. Afterwards, on the Serpentine Bridge, she gave me her blistering review. *Superficially flashy*, she said, squeezing my hand in sympathy. Levelling her grey eyes at me, she made me promise to live a more daring life; to do whatever it took to match my skill with lucid, authentic feeling.

Annie's candour was dizzying. A rope in my mind came loose from its moorings, nimbly unhitched by her words. She knew that I had taken refuge in a narrow existence, trying to hide the clumsiness that had grown so pronounced under my parents' pitying gaze. I am ugly, you see. Not just in a particular light, or in the eyes of certain beholders. My aspect is irrefutably displeasing, and all attempts to say otherwise quickly fade into hopeless mumbling. Still, Annie tried to guide my terrified hand to life's tiller. It was because of her that my fears eventually gave way to hope. And after that, adventure.

When we emerged onto Regent Street in the heat of that sticky London summer, I was more wilted and gangly than ever, while Annie, as if travelling some other-worldly draught of air, was fresh as a lark at dawn. Stalking for birthday treasure, we made Liberty our quarry. Annie was bright-eyed as a child who'd passed through the looking glass, sifting eagerly through jewel coloured silks and delighting in the wheeze of perfume diffusers. By the time we left for my tatty rooms in Marylebone, she was taking it all in her stride. There was a green foulard knotted about her head like a turban and the silage of Mitsouko rolled off it in narcotic waves. My sister was self-possessed; dauntless. It was little wonder that I looked to her when, as was so often the case, the strength of my own convictions failed.

There will be no galvanizing flash of Annie's viridian silk today. I had hoped that its liquid flow might grant me the power to change certain parts of my life as I have lived them in the wake of that sultry afternoon; reprise the theme with greater dash before my performance reaches its coda. But the scarf is no longer numinous in my nephew's eyes. I have deconsecrated it by inserting myself in the picture.

'We're just back from Paris,' Stella chirps. 'They had these huge barges on the river with mountains of sand on them to make beaches ... '

Terence can always rely on his wife's forced airiness to avoid meaningful conversation. She twirls one of Maggie's thin, slippery braids with her fingers. To her other side, Iris pitches herself against her mother's shoulder and slumps in a defeated heap. I watch as both children drift into a trance of boredom. Fixed on the nothingness of the middle distance, their eyes grow round and glassy. My thumb and middle finger tense, ready to snap them back to attention. But my Aunt Katherine, stern and stout, surveys us from a photograph on top of the piano, and I can't summon the audacity to express my outrage in front of her.

Katherine never looked young. She is no more than fifty-years old in this picture, but her hair is set in stiff curls and her thick ankles bulge over the sides of her patent shoes. She is wearing her customary floral dress, buttoned to the neck, the massive roses disguising any shape beneath their tangle. I used to read her face as blank—bovine even—but recently, I have divined something new in her expression. The directness of her gaze is arch. And the thin line of her mouth seems subtly shrewd.

Behind her is Lusillaun House, black mould sprawling beneath its gutters and sills, yew trees crowded tight against its downstairs windows. Our father took a detour to visit Katherine in this dishevelled pile on the way to Dingle every summer, causing Annie and me to send up wild laments. The house frightened us, filled as it was with the trappings of her loneliness—the greasy mark that her head had made on the solitary chair by the fireplace, the stale biscuits that broke into mealy clods on our tongues, the bob of the pendulum as it rocked relentlessly in the clock case, marching her closer to what we imagined—or even hoped to be—her imminent death. We were unsentimental about Aunt Katherine. She was a cloud passing over our sun, a cold shadow to be endured before the delirium of summer.

I remember so little about her from those early visits; practically nothing except for the broad outline of a woman who remarked upon my massive hands as I sat upon her couch one day. *The poor child*, she said, adding *God bless the mark* on a rasping inhalation. Never, before or since, have my hands felt so devastatingly huge—like balloons, buoyant and irrepressible, on the ends of my arms. I loathed her for this mortification, for causing my pulse to pound until my livid cheeks ached. But she wasn't blind to my suffering. *They're a pianist's hands*, she said, by way of balm. *Like Rachmaninoff's*. After that, I grew curious about the hammering of metal strings, and I learned how to transfigure my shame into a kind of glory.

I nudge Katherine's silver-framed figure around until she can see into the room, sharing my appalling vantage. Stella is holding forth about pectin and runny jam and Terence will not meet my eyes. Finding them too beady and full of inquiry, he ignores me as one might a dissident toddler. The skin of his neck is slack, I notice. Fat has softened the once-sharp line of his jaw. I was not long back from London when my own jowls made their appearance; dire proof that my features were not yet complete in their delinquency. I had convinced myself that I was on sabbatical, though I knew I would never return to my former life. Not after my splendid man had rejected me. For over a decade, every moment of our love had been astonishing to me; as if a butterfly, weightless and crystalline, had come to rest on my finger and a careless breath might drive it away. When he told me that his restive passion for me had ended, I grew numb; became one of life's blunt instruments. It left me a ghost in the making, a scar in space and time. With my last breath, I believe that my spirit will burst free and make passage across the Irish Sea to Montagu Square, to the place where we two parted. Lately, I feel it rattle at the cage of my chest, determined to take flight and finally grieve its fill.

Home was no longer Regency Marylebone when Annie called to say Katherine was gone, but rather the fourth floor of a Leeson Street hotel. We shared a sombre pause on the phone; a respectful silence filled with half-hearted grief. Then Annie delivered some further news. Our aunt, alleging to be of sound mind, had named us her sole heirs. I heard my sister's lips peel from her gums and teeth as she smiled broadly with amusement, waiting for my reaction.

I thought of Lusillaun, empty in the darkness, and imagined it to be waiting for us. In a fit of romance, I begged Annie to come and get me. The idea of driving there was the only diversion for my misery and, although she protested loudly, she folded for a bottle of Boodles gin. We'd never taken the journey as adults. Along the way, blasts of dewy air and silage fed our nostalgia, tempered by the smoke from our Pall Malls. When we arrived, the house was stark against dawn's opaline sheen, asleep under the spell of stasis cast by Katherine's old age. Convinced that my aunt had never seen the potential of its pitch pine floors, declining orangery or teasing glimpses of lake water beyond the meadow, I set out to rescue it—to erase her. By the time sunlight purled in the flaws of the west windows, every grimy pelmet was down, every shutter was opened, and my arms were criss-crossed with glistening furrows ploughed by the needles of the axe-felled yews.

Annie had little forbearance as she watched me cleave to Lusillaun, not realising that my promise to her was being fulfilled. If only she could hear my Fauré now. What I lack in crisp articulation I make up for in spectacular remoteness. It is a kind of ventriloquism on the keyboard, full of the distant shimmer of the life I once had.

Stella drones on and Maggie is mock-sleeping, head thrown back with mouth open, as comically sullen as her grandmother was when she was young. Iris smirks, delighted by her sister's mischief, just as I used to be proud of Annie's. No doubt they think themselves the original of the species and live in dread of resemblance to anyone who has come before them. Yet I relish seeing these echoes in them, with all of the peculiar sadness and bitterness that goes with any one-sided attachment. To the children, I am nothing more than a farting cushion and a pair of monumental hands. A chill winter that they wish would give way to spring.

'Why don't you go into the garden, girls?' I whisper, conspiratorial.

They are like greyhounds out of a trap, a snarl of elbows and knees before they vanish into the hall. When they reappear in the meadow, it is as a different class of creature; spirited, vital, Iris's laughter pealing while Maggie pantomimes a monster across the choked flowerbeds.

I never brought this house back from its brink. It always ran from my grasp, its entropy outpacing me at every turn. But as I watch the girls' silhouettes descend towards the lake, I grow certain of one thing. This glorious pair must have Lusillaun. Imagine what they might do with it.

The Day I Met Vini Reilly
by Will Kemp

Vini isn't exactly an international celebrity, but when he's loved, he's very very loved
Tony Wilson, Factory Records

I can't remember what I was doing on hearing about 9/11, but I do remember the first time I heard the Durutti Column. It happened aged sixteen, on a visit to London with a friend during the Easter holidays. Ostensibly the trip was made to see the plays we were doing for English A-level, but all we learnt that week was how to get served in a pub and what we saw in the sex cinemas of Soho.

Killing time one afternoon in Leicester Square, we bounced into a record shop to see what they had. And there, all around, was *the* most beautiful sound—neither rock nor classical, yet somehow both of them too—a haunting, atmospheric guitar, delicate and intricate, rising and falling, with distant vocals, piano and drums. I'd never heard anything like it before. I had to have it.

'Er, excuse me, what's this you're playing?' I asked the assistant at the counter.

'The Durutti Column.'

'The what?'

'The Durutti Column. A guitarist called Vini Reilly and another fella. Factory Records. Manchester.'

'Factory?'

'Yep. Same label as Joy Division, but totally different sound.'

'And what's this record called?'

'*LC.*'

'*Elsie?*'

'L.C. Short for Lotta Continua. Latin for *the struggle goes on* or something like that.'

Cool.

'And what is the Durutti Column? Is that Roman too?'

'Dunno. I'll get you the cover.'

He turned to a library of record sleeves then handed me an album cover. It was white, with squiggles of red and orange watercolour. Beautiful, sensitive and different. Just like the music.

'Have they done anything else?'

'Yeah. Two albums. *Another Setting*, and er, *The Return of the Durutti Column*.'

As he went to fetch these, I studied the track titles from *LC*. *Sketch for Dawn*. *Portrait for Frazer*. *Detail for Paul*. They must have gone to art school. Cool indeed.

'Here you go,' he said, placing the other two before me.

'I'll have all three, please,' I said, blowing the last of my pocket money as well as the chance of seeing any more sex films in Soho.

And I suppose I knew even then that the Durutti were better than sex.

Time moves on and yet stands still. Twenty-two years in fact. University follows school, girlfriends come and go, the Tories replace Labour, Labour replaces the Tories, the mullett supercedes the feather cut, and is itself superceded by any number of styles facilitated by the advent of hair gel. I even become a planner.

But during this time of change, one thing remains steadfast—the enduring brilliance of the Durutti Column. I buy every LP, then every CD, playing them over and over, never once tiring of Vini's distinctive, heavenly sound, sure it is ahead of its time and yet timeless too.

Inadvertently he thereby provides the soundtrack for my life. He is there when I fall in love, when I score my first century, when I lose my virginity. And he is there too when love breaks down, when my parents die, always understanding the loss with his poignant, stabbing guitar.

And all the time I wait for that special girl who will love the Durutti too.

The only scratch on the Ming vase is that I never see them in concert. But then they never did much stuff *live*. And they were *Factory Records* (so-called because so many factories were closing in Manchester that founder Tony Wilson liked the idea of one opening). *Factory* were hip and *alternative*, relying on word of mouth. So whilst non-Manc-me never stood a chance of hearing about any of their gigs, Vini's fine music also remained largely unknown.

But then God invents the internet (and God must exist, because how else would Vini exist?), and I discover the Durutti are playing in Manchester. Within five minutes, I have bought two tickets and feel dizzy with excitement: at long last, twenty-two years after walking into that record shop off Leicester Square, I am actually going to see Vini *live*.

My friend Pete drives. Pete is stocky, dependable and rosy-faced, like a favourite uncle. By day he works as an environmental scientist, by night he plays drums in a gypsy rock band; he thereby shares a certain dualism in being both an environmental professional and an *artiste de demain*.

I've invited him because I owe him favours and because he is a musician, so his opinion is sound and matters—matters, that is, unless he thinks Vini is crap, in which case he doesn't know anything and can get lost. Moreover, he is from Manchester and happy to drive, meaning that we can go straight to the venue (Comedy Store, Deansgate Locks); this is critical, because we can't be late and I need to be free to take in the object of my veneration (adoration, love, obsession).

Outside, the Pennine landscape of the M62 passes by in long hill hauls, with signs to Huddersfield and Halifax, bare moors and windswept reservoirs, the surface waters choppy with waves under a grey sky.

It is not raining, but I want it too. I want Manchester to be Manchester, with storm clouds over dark mills, to be part of the melancholy that has inspired Vini's ethereal, often wistful, sound.

I feel tense but excited, like a child going to see a lion at the zoo. I hope there will be a full house, with some good-looking women, one of whom could be that special. I hope there will be some Durutti T-shirts on sale too so as to proclaim my allegiance to the Blessed One. And with the excitement come butterflies in my stomach in case we are late, Vini is ill or the hippie organisers have cocked up with the date...

A sign for Rochdale flits by. This is Vini country, I think, recalling that *Les Preger's Tune* off the album *Vini Reilly* was a homage to a neighbour there who fought for the communists during the Spanish Civil War.

I wonder what it must be like to have Vini dedicate a track to you, musing how he would surely dedicate something to me if we met—because there's always been that connection between us, just the two of us, as if he had created all that unique, angelic music just for arty, sensitive me.

And I wonder how the drab houses and post-industrial dereliction massing the hills around us relate to his music which always conjures autumnal mists and colours, the innocence of childhood. It is easy to think of his music as an escape, that his life too has been one more dreamed than lived.

And so to Manchester. Thanks to my fear of being late, we are four hours early. Four hours early but twenty-two years late. It is a Sunday afternoon, late April. There is not much traffic, and it is raining slightly. Not hard rain, but soft and slow—a steady drizzle of feathery rain—the same rain that created the textiles industry and the sense of melancholy that pervades so much of Vini's music.

But it is only when I see a poster with the word 'Durutti' that I know we have arrived.

The venue is deserted. We wander into a spacious hall with refurbished brick walls, a wooden floor and a giant TV screen at one end. It feels like the departure lounge of a small airport, and I clutch onto our £15 tickets like passports.

On the screen, without sound, is an old man in a crumpled linen suit behind a drum kit and a diminutive figure with a guitar and a haircut I recognise from the album cover of *Sex and Death*.

'My God,' I murmur, 'it's him.'

'What—the band?' asks Pete. 'But there's only two of them.'

'There *are* only two of them.'

'Oh. Well, they'll be doing the sound check. In the main auditorium. But look at what he's doing, the guitarist —he's showing the drummer how to play! Look at 'im!'

I look at Vini, and sure enough he is instructing drummer Bruce Mitchell on what Bruce surely knows best...

The image confirms the perfectionism I have always suspected, and makes me wonder if Vini is, in his own little way, a control freak too—bursting into rages at bum notes, and more besides. I doubt it. The creator of such gentle music could hardly be a total arsehole.

Relief. Vini is not ill. And he's not doing keyboards only. The organisers have come good with the date. It's on, and I'm here. And who knows, with us being so early, I might even be able to meet him...

We sit down on a big black sofa, watching Vini's silent cameo performance above. Occasionally people pop in and out of camera shot, until there is no more movement.

The sound-check must be over. The little genius might walk in to the hall at any second.

Sure enough, a little figure with dark hair walks in by the end wall towards the bar area. It is Vini Reilly.

I go cold inside. This is my chance to speak to him, but I have no idea what to say. I feel hollow, sixteen again, a gangly schoolboy freezing in front of the school honey for whom I have spent all week preparing and rehearsing a chat-up line that is now lost in the trembling moment of meeting.

But I have to see him, thank him... I may never get another chance.

Though what if he is heading for the Gents? What to do then? Accost him there? Wait outside even?

He stops at the end of the bar to join a solid-looking woman and a man with a long grey ponytail. They look pleased to see him and start talking.

It is now or never.

I begin the long walk, in slow motion it seems, my head turning over with possible lines. *I want to thank you... I just want to thank you... I just want to say how thankful I am...*

I reach the group, a yard away now from my all-time hero.

The conversation stops, and Vini looks up at me humbly, guiltily, like a street urchin awaiting sentence for some trivial theft. His face is gaunt and dry, its chiselled features gnarled and twisted, like a wooden sculpture—the nose hispanic or roman, his dimples suction-packed, the wild hair ashen and gypsy-like. He reminds me of Keith Richards, only smaller and more unhealthy—a young waif and an old crone at the same time, the neck painfully thin and extending like a tortoise's, his tiny body a withered weed by the roadside.

'Er, hello,' I rattle, extending a hand. 'Can I buy you— buy you all—a coffee or something?'

'No, it's OK,' he says out the corner of his mouth, his hand weak in mine, his voice soft as the rain outside.

There is a horrible silence as I wish I had prepared something to say—and did not sound so posh, and was not so tall. In fact I tower over Vini, looking down on the man I look up to. For the first time in my life I sense how threatening my height is, and want to be small.

The man with the ponytail gives me a dismissive look. But Vini and the large woman seem to know this is an important rite of passage, and calmly await my next line.

'Look,' I continue, slouching in an attempt to reduce my height. 'This is more embarrassing for me than it is for you...'

Vini continues his defensive upward stare at me—his dark eyes seeming to get bigger and bigger, like a cartoon owl—his head tilted forward in concentration as— unbelievably—*he* listens to *me*.

'...But I just want to thank you for all the colour and enrichment your music has put into my life—'

'No, no,' interrupts the minuscule giant, gently. 'Thank *you* for buying the records.'

The comment is genuine, and takes my breath away. I swallow hard, conscious of the need to say something, to keep the sacred flame of conversation alive.

'You see, I've been a fan for twenty-two years now, and well, I've never seen you *live*. And I'm really excited. About tonight, I mean. Because after all those years I'm going to see you *live*... So I really hope it goes well for you. Tonight, I mean.'

The jumbled words tumble out of me, and trail off.

'Thank you.'

I pause, dumbstruck, noticing how big his veins are— or rather how thin his arms are. He has the emaciated look of a vegan, vagrant or drug addict—and maybe all three—as if a cough or sneeze would be enough to blow him away. He must be ill, I think, wanting to nurse him back to health, wrap him in cotton wool.

'Excuse me, but I need to go for a fag,' he says, looking to break out of the tall circle around him.

'Yes, yes, of course. Well, look, good luck tonight. And cheers.'

'Cheers,' he says as he passes by, so close I feel the faint rush of his cigarette breath on my face.

I stay where I am, elated and dazed, like a prisoner of war blinking with disbelief at freedom, relieved too Vini has a sweet nature—just as I always hoped and imagined. I ponder his words and treasure his earnest look at me, amazed that *he thanked me*.

And then I think of the hundred questions I should have asked him—which is his favourite album, where does he go shopping, can I buy him—them—a meal before the gig...

I turn animated to a bemused Pete, raising my arms aloft as if I had just taken ten wickets.

'Pete! I've spoken to him, I've spoken to him!'

'I can see that!' Pete laughs, shaking his head.

I shut my eyes in joy and relief and disbelief. I have got to have a beer to celebrate. Several in fact.

By the time we roll in to the back of the auditorium, the supporting act—a singer from Africa—is finishing hers. When she does, the place empties for a drink before the main event, thereby freeing up seats. We descend to the middle block, and like a pair of vultures shamelessly occupy the best seats in the house—five rows back from the main microphone.

Pete talks me through the electronics and angle of the jazz drums, and I take notes, acting the part of a freelance journalist in case anyone challenges us for *their* seats. Nobody does, though when the place starts to refill I notice out of the corner of my eye the ousted couple lamely accepting their misfortune.

Just as I am thinking things cannot get any better, the large woman from earlier sits down next to me.

'Oh hello,' I smile. 'I met you earlier. Are you family, friend or another musician?'

'I'm Carol,' she replies, 'his partner of the last five years.'

'My God! That's amazing! Look, I'm sorry about earlier... It's embarrassing, but I'm such a big fan –'

'Oh, don't worry, you're OK. It happens quite a lot.'

I pause, taking it in.

'What's he like?' I ask, unable to contain myself.

'Pretty much as you'd think he is, I suppose.'

'What, you mean quiet and sensitive? Couldn't harm a fly?'

'That's it,' she says thoughtfully, as if acknowledging the importance of the question. 'But he can be a real bastard. He woke up this morning—I was still sleeping—and said, can you think of a fish beginning with the letter H? So we lay there, for over an hour, trying to think of all the fish beginning with an H…'

She explains that sometimes he will stay up all night if he has a tune in his head, and relates how a few years ago he was in real financial trouble after the break-up of Factory. I start to think of how I can help. I give her my business card, and promise to see if I can help promote Vini (in London via DJ friend at XFM Radio), throwing in an improbable offer of free planning advice for good measure.

'Oh thank you,' she says, taken aback, as if I have offered her the crown jewels.

'No, no,' I reply, Vini-style. '*Thank you.*'

Vini appears on stage, alone and uncertain, a guitar strapped across his shoulder, and stumbles towards the microphone amid a rapturous reception that he looks uncomfortable with.

'This is for the nice man I met earlier at the bar,' I want to hear him say.

'Hello,' he mumbles instead. 'Thanks for coming. Hope you enjoy the music. This one's for my niece who's here tonight. It's called *Spasmic Fairy*.'

Vini has never had the gift of track titles. In fact, I cannot think of a more unlikely rock star—but when he plays, he plays. And as he does, the audience is still, spellbound, drawn towards some other Hamlyn, stupefied at how quickly his long fingernails can pluck notes from a guitar, as all the angels of heaven settle amongst the stage lights to wonder at the sound rising below.

This is the first track I have heard the Vinmeister play live, and although not a favourite, it has been worth the wait. I wonder if he will play anything from *LC*, or ask for someone to help out on guitar while he plays keyboards, picturing myself on stage with him, innocuously strumming an acoustic guitar. It is not the first time I know I have missed my true vocation or wished I could play.

The second track is also instrumental, the third another solo partly accompanied by his *sotto* vocals.

It is only with the fourth that Old Man Mitchell appears, to delirious applause, and begins to slap the drum intro to *The Missing Boy* as if warding off a host of evil spirits.

As Vini delivers the virtuoso chords, he becomes bigger and bigger. The light shines bright on his red shirt, creating a purple blue shadow under the strap anchoring guitar to shoulder. My head and body move to the irrepressible rhythm, transported, mouthing the words I know so well in time to the ghostly wail of Vini's voice.

I think I am in love with Vini. Not the love for a partner but the love for a kid brother. I see him as a puny outsider in the playground, the music class nerd, picked on and bullied, a Mancunian Kes—someone who needs a good bath and a square meal inside him… And suddenly I want to stand up and smash their heads in, the bullies I have never seen—because nobody's going to come near my little Vin and hurt him.

He plays and plays, and I listen, hoping he will play twenty-two tracks to make up for the missing years—a kind of Durutti royal gun salute.

But in the end he looks shattered, and the band's sound descends into an untypical wall of noise. I am sure it is *avant garde*, but I want him off-stage in case he becomes ill or harms his chances of getting a record deal from someone in the crowd…

Besides, I have realised a dream, Vini has lived up to an ideal, the gig is over.

En route home, I am on a drug-free high—and struggle to take it all in. It has been a perfect day, better than I could have hoped for. Not only to have seen the Durutti live, but to have met Vini, and thanked him, sat next to his girlfriend even. I feel I've known him all my life. And I suppose I have, really.

They were brilliant, he was fantastic. But even if they'd been crap, they'd still have been brilliant.

£15 a ticket? I'd have paid £1,500.

'I'm really pleased for you, Will,' says Pete as the street lights flash by. 'I've never seen you so happy. But you've got to learn guitar. You'd get so much out of it…'

He is probably right, but I am not really listening. I am looking out the window slightly open-mouthed, thinking about all the different kinds of fish beginning with H.

Jane Austin, born in Liverpool, is retired from the University of York. Her first novel, *News from Nowhere*, will be published by Cinnamon, spring 2017. A keen linguist and walker, Jane lives with her husband and cats in York.

Jennifer Bailey grew up in Lancashire and gradually travelled south. She taught at a series of universities including Leicester, Nottingham, California State in Sacramento and London's City University. The serious writing took hold recently and a number of stories have been published in *Slow Dancer, The New Writer, Fish Anthology, Staple,* and by Cinnamon Press. A novella, *Pictures of Margaret,* was runner-up in Manchester Metropolitan Uni

Rosa Valerie Campbell is originally from Sydney and now lives in London. This year her work has featured in *The Letters Page, Litro, I am because you are anthology* (Freight Press) *East End Literary Salon, nomfiction anthology* (Big Truths), *Feminartsy* and Noted Festival. She's just finished a novel. @rrrosavalerie

Aoife Fitzpatrick lives and works in Dublin, and studied at the School of English, Trinity College. Her short stories have been recognised by several international short-story competitions, including the Seán Ó'Faoláin Prize and the *Australian Book Review*'s Elizabeth Jolley Prize. Her work has been published by the literary journal *Southword.*

Mandy Huggins's travel writing and short fiction has appeared in anthologies, newspapers and magazines. She has achieved success in numerous competitions, including New Writer, Fish, Ink Tears, English Pen, The Telegraph, Bradt, and Words with Jam. In 2014 she won the British Guild of Travel Writers New Travel Writer Award.

Will Kemp studied at Cambridge and UEA before working as an environmental planner. He has won or been highly placed in several competitions His first collection, *Nocturnes*, was published by Cinnamon in 2011 and *Lowland*, was published in 2013. *The Painters Who Studied Clouds* will be published in 2015.

Kathryn Lund is a MA writing student at Oxford Brookes. Her work, both poetry and short story, frequently explores her own experiences of neurological problems and treatment. 'Whatever Happened' was developed from issues of compulsion and disappearance as well as observations from therapy. She sometimes reads at Oxford poetry events.

Jane McLaughlin writes poetry and fiction. She completed the Cinnamon Press mentoring programme in 2014. Her stories have been published in Cinnamon Press anthologies and in *The Frogmore Papers* and *Under the Radar*. Her poetry collection, *Lockdown*, will be published by Cinnamon in autumn 2016.

Kate Mitchell completed the MA in Writing at Sheffield Hallam University and is the author of a novel, *The House Fell on Her Head*. It has been said that Kate's writing explores the darker side of human nature, possibly a reflection of a life spent working in the penal system.

L F Roth's short stories have appeared in competition anthologies published by Biscuit Publishing (2011), Earlyworks Press (2012, 2012-13, 2014) and Bridge House Publishing (2014), as well as on the web (Segora, 2012). They generally focus on relationships, gender issues and trauma—at times all three.

Jeremy Worman's second collection, *Swimming with Diana Dors and Other Stories*, was published by Cinnamon Press in 2014. He has reviewed for *The Observer*, the *Times Literary Supplement* and many other publications. He has degrees in English from London University and Cambridge University and is now working on a memoir as a practice-based PhD at Goldsmiths. www.jeremyworman.com